To
JUANITA

OTHER TITLES BY DIANA PULLEIN-THOMPSON
IN THE ARMADA SERIES INCLUDE

A PONY FOR SALE
THE PENNYFIELDS
JANET MUST RIDE
HORSES AT HOME
RIDING WITH THE LYNTONS
I WANTED A PONY

A Pony to School was first published in
the U.K. in 1950 by William Collins
Sons & Co., Ltd, London and Glasgow.
This edition was first published in 1963
by May Fair Books Ltd, 14 St. James's
Place, London, S.W.1, and was printed in
Great Britain by Love & Malcomson Ltd,
Brighton Road, Redhill, Surrey.

DIANA PULLEIN-THOMPSON

A Pony to School

COVER ILLUSTRATION
BY PETER ARCHER;

TEXT ILLUSTRATIONS
BY ANNE BULLEN

Armada

Clown waked from his daydreaming with a start

Chapter 1 by Christina

IT WAS Saturday afternoon, and that meant a rest from school work and Madame Dupont, the governess who teaches Augusta and myself.

Usually, Augusta and I spend Saturdays riding—taking sandwiches if the weather is fine and picnicking far from home—or occasionally we spend the morning schooling and jumping the ponies, and the afternoon walking our dogs, a spaniel and a wolfhound, called Lucifer and Shannan.

But on this day in late June, fresh and beautiful with its alternate sunshine and showers, our usual arrangement was changed by a visit from a nearby farmer, named Ted Dunne. I was on the lawn, reading the morning paper, when he arrived, and I started at Walters' quiet, "Someone to speak to you, miss." Then, seeing a hefty man of about thirty standing before me looking hard at his wellington boots, I was filled with curiosity. What could he want? The ponies had not strayed lately; in fact they were all stabled at present; and Shannan was not in the habit of hunting or trespassing. With relief, I decided that he had not come to complain.

"Good morning," I said, dropping the paper and leaping to my feet. "Lovely weather, isn't it?"

"Yes, it is that," replied Ted Dunne slowly, pushing a lock of hair back from his forehead. "Are you busy-like at the moment—I mean with your 'orses?"

"No, not very," I said, mystified.

Ted Dunne pondered for a few seconds before saying, " 'Ave you time for another?"

"We don't want to buy any more at present—at least my parents don't," I answered cautiously.

"Ever trained one?"

"No, not completely."

"Yours win a lot, though, don't they? Carry off all the ribbons?"

"I wouldn't say *all*. They've been awfully good and obliging this summer so far; but still, probably it won't last. I shall fall off at the next show and upset them for the rest of the year, or something silly," I said, wondering all the while what this man really wanted.

"Like to 'ave a shot at training one?" he asked.

"Yes, if my parents would allow it."

"I've got a lovely skewbald—real beauty, if it 'ad the right rider on it—prettily marked, quick on its feet—real smasher."

"Are you trying to sell it?" I asked.

"No—be a waste, selling 'im now. 'E's not schooled-like, you see; but if *you* 'ad 'im for a week or two—trained 'im up a bit—huh! there would be no getting near that pony, no touching 'im. 'E would carry off all the prizes. Used to jumping a bit, too."

"Can I see him before I decide anything definite, please?" I asked.

"Certainly, whenever you like. 'E's laying out. I'm somewhere about the farm most days." When he finished speaking, Ted Dunne raised his head, looked me in the face for one fleeting second and then turned as though to go.

"Wait a sec., please," I said. "Where do you live and what exactly do you want me to do with the pony?"

"Why, down at Beech Bottom Farm—but a couple of miles from 'ere—stands almost in the wood like. You come and look at the pony—Clown, we calls 'im —when it's convenient, see; p'raps we can get everything settled then."

"Righto, I will. Thank you very much," I said, and

6

then Ted Dunne plodded away and I returned to my chair for a few moments to collect my wits and consider his vague and unexpected request.

Of course everything depended on Clown, I decided. I had always wanted to break in or school a pony, but I did not think that I had enough skill to tackle a difficult or vicious one with any success. Then I thought of my friend Augusta, who possesses more tact and imagination, if less experience, than myself. The two of us might succeed where I alone would fail. I decided to ring her up.

I got through in a few minutes and, although at first she was a little dubious, I think Augusta was really very pleased with the suggestion.

"Skewbald? Sounds lovely," she said. "I should love to help; it would be tremendous fun and excellent for improving my riding; but are you sure I'm good enough?"

"If I am, you certainly are," I replied rather sharply, because Augusta's modesty is sometimes a little irritating. "And I don't want you to *help* me, please; I want you to come into partnership—not that we are getting any money. I mean I gather we are doing it for experience and fun."

"Oh, well, thank you very much. I should love to. What's he called? What does he look like? Has he ever been ridden at all?"

When I had finished repeating Ted Dunne's conversation, Augusta invited me to ride over for elevenses to Bumpers, which is the name of the little Georgian farmhouse where the Thorndykes live, to discuss Clown and to decide on which day we should see him.

I accepted the invitation gladly. I always enjoy myself at Bumpers, and there is something indescribably homely about the snack they call elevenses. I remembered now, lingering in our hall, the last time I had been there; how we climbed the trees in their little sprawling orchard and later sat on a fallen trunk and ate huge hunks of warm new bread and fresh yellow

7

cheese, and drank cool cider, which seemed to taste not only of apples but of sunshine and the red soil of Somerset.

And I remembered how one day we had wandered into the brick-floored kitchen and talked to old Martha, as she prepared the lunch of cheese eggs, and apple tart. Martha does not put herself out to be polite. If she is busy, she will soon tell you to be off to the nursery or orchard, but sometimes, when the world seems right with her, she will tell you stories of past employers or you will learn that long ago in the days of Martha's childhood many country children were brought up on potatoes and bread and never tasted chocolate or cream. These stories used to horrify me. On the particular day that I remembered now, she described how she and her sister at the ages of nine and ten used to walk a mile to draw water from a well and toil home with full buckets. I never wondered whether these stories were true; it was just pleasant to hang about the kitchen and hear them. At home I am not really allowed in the servants' quarters, and Walters and Cook never tell me anything interesting, and Mummy seems to arrange the menu. But Augusta is always tasting the dishes and persuading Martha to make pancakes or something special for tea.

It was with these pleasant memories in my mind that I went whistling down to the stables. My three ponies—Symphony, Solo and Serenade—had finished their breakfast and were looking over their loose-box doors. Serenade's head, bay and starred, was on the left, then Solo's, dark brown like a coffee bean, and on the very right was Symphony's golden head. They looked like a calendar—gazing into the early sunlight with pricked ears—and suddenly I thought how very lucky I was to possess such agreeable and beautiful ponies. They are all so nice and so different from each other, I told myself. And I patted the three sleek, firm necks in turn and tried to decide which pony I should ride over to Bumpers.

Presently I decided to take Serenade, because he seems to enjoy being ridden more than the other two. On fine days he bangs at his door and whinnies hopefully, as though he expects to be taken out. I thought that he would be sorry to miss the sunshine this morning; although later it would probably be too hot for his liking.

After telling O'Neil, who looks after my ponies and was at that moment cutting chaff in the forage-room, and Mummy of my intentions, I saddled and bridled Serenade and, calling Shannan, rode down the drive to the road and then out into Foxey Lane, which is shaded by high banks, green with nettles and meadowsweet, and thick leafy hedges. A light breeze blew on my face; little skittish clouds raced across the blue sky; cows grazed peacefully in the small sheltered fields; perched on the branch of a giant oak, a thrush sang bravely and alone. His light-heartedness was catching; in a moment I too was singing.

When I turned into the road it started to rain, but by the time I had reached Bumpers the sun was shining once more and I found everything as I had expected. Augusta, dark, small and slim, was sitting on the doorstep shelling peas, and watching a bantam and chicks scratching in the drive; Lucifer was beside her. Hearing my hoofbeats, she sprang to her feet, upsetting a pile of pods, and came running round to the stable, which is long and low and made of bricks and flints, and helped me unsaddle Serenade.

"What about seeing Clown this afternoon?" she suggested.

"I suppose there's no reason why we shouldn't," I said.

We went out into the orchard and climbed up a tree, and, sitting astride a bough, ate whiteheart cherries and bread and cheese, and made plans. Daybreak, Augusta's grey pony gelding, wandered lazily across the wet grass and stood, looking up at us in the hope that we would throw him down some bread. Lucifer clawed at the trunk of the tree. And still the sun shone with all the golden warmth of June.

We decided to see Ted Dunne and Clown that very afternoon. Augusta was surprised that I had not found out more about the skewbald. She wanted to know his age and whether he had a long mane and tail and whether he was sound in wind, limb and eye; soon I realised that I had been very inefficient, but the fact that we knew so little about the pony seemed to make our venture all the more exciting.

Augusta gave her imagination full rein, and presently we saw ourselves hunting a part arab skewbald pony with a flowing mane and tail and the most beautiful manners, jumping enormous fences. I was, in my mind's eye, approaching a formidable brook behind the master of our local pack of foxhounds, when we heard angry cries in the garden.

"Gosh, what on earth is happening?" wondered Augusta. And the next moment Shannan appeared over the orchard gate with a shoulder of mutton in his mouth, followed by a furious Martha. Augusta tried to leap from her bough and fell into a bed of nettles. I slithered down the trunk, scraping my knees, and ran to the rescue. Shannan dropped the joint quickly enough, but before we had gathered our wits together, Lucifer had seized the prize and, carrying it proudly in his jaws, made off into the woods.

"That's put the cork in the bottle," said Augusta.

"What an awful phrase. Can't you catch him?" I asked. She whistled without success. Then Martha, trembling and short of breath, reached us.

"Oh, those wicked dogs; they'll be the death of me," she cried. "He took it off the table, right in front of my nose."

Feeling very guilty, I apologised profusely and scolded Shannan, who put on a sorrowful expression but persisted in wagging his long grey tail.

"It was for to-night," said Martha, "for dinner—and now what are we to 'ave?"

We ran to the edge of the wood, calling Lucifer, but in vain. We were still calling when Mrs. Thornedyke arrived back from a shopping expedition. We explained all and she was very decent and treated our dogs' bad behaviour more as a joke than anything else, and calmed the rightly indignant Martha. Then I told her about Clown, and suggested that Augusta should ride over with me and have lunch at Hampton House and that we would go down to Beech Bottom Farm during the afternoon. As every one thought this was a sensible suggestion, we caught and groomed Daybreak and, after I had apologised again for Shannan's barbarism and said how much I enjoyed the elevenses, we started for home.

Because the ponies were fresh and the sun was shining, we rode back through the woods and across the springy green turf of the common, which was once a golf course. We talked of the approaching horse shows and gymkhanas. Chilswood was the only one for which we had entered so far. It was going to be held on Bank Holiday, and Augusta hoped to ride Daybreak in the Children's Jumping, the Pony Showing, the Open Bending, the Open Potato and the V.C. Race, and I hoped to ride all my three ponies in the Children's Jumping, Symphony in the Pony Showing, and Solo in the three races. We both secretly wondered whether Clown would be schooled in time to compete. It was just over five weeks to Bank Holiday.

Chapter 2 by Augusta

HAMPTON HOUSE is one of those lovely stucco houses of the Regency period, with long windows, white pillars, white steps and a balcony boasting a beautiful, delicately wrought-iron balustrade. For years it had belonged to the Folley family, the youngest of which—twins, Heather and Pat—are members of the same riding club as Christina and me. I like Hampton House; I like its elegance, its lavish decoration, its air of luxury and comfort. I like the garden too, which I am told is earlier than the house, the box hedges trimly enclosing the borders, the soft sweep of lawns, the cool dark cedars and the more humble trees with mossy roots; and, of course, I like the peaches and the plums, the nectarines and grapes, which linger on the walls or cluster in the hot-houses. But Christina insists that the whole place has an unfriendly atmosphere, and she says that, whether in the garden or the house, she feels like a guest—almost an intruder. She thinks that there is some part of the Folleys left behind, that their laughter rang for too long in the long light passages, that their feet trod too often the rose-scented paths. She believes that, although her father sows new lawns, constructs tennis courts, cuts down, with growing enthusiasm, the Victorian shrubberies, the deep impression made by four generations of strong-minded Folleys will never fade.

I remembered Christina's pessimistic views on this July day and, turning the corner in the drive to see the house—so magnificent and white in the dazzling sunlight—made me wish that the Carrs were a larger family.

"Well, here we are," said Christina, "and we had better hurry. O'Neil will be having lunch and we are late for ours, and Cook and Mummy will be fussing. Can you shove Daybreak in the spare box?"

The ponies settled, we ran indoors, washed our hands and ate a delicious meal. Walters waited at table; Mrs. Carr made suitable conversation. Everything was very stiff and proper, and I felt foolish and self-conscious and hardly uttered a word.

We were not allowed to ride down to Beech Bottom Farm at once, because Mrs. Carr said we must digest our food properly. We had to sit still for ten minutes and read books, which was all right normally, but rather tiresome when you were dying to see a new pony. Presently, however, she allowed us to go and we rushed and saddled Symphony and Serenade— Christina very kindly said that I could ride Symphony, a chestnut mare of rather uncertain temper, who has won countless prizes in showing classes—and in a very short time we were trotting slowly through the beech woods.

Ted Dunne was taking an afternoon nap in the farmhouse when we arrived, and came out wearing breeches, gaiters and a leather waistcoat. After hearing that we wanted to see Clown, he went back indoors and fetched himself a coat before hurrying us down to a vast rough field, at the end of which, beneath a magnificent chestnut tree, stood a skewbald pony swishing his long dirty-white tail.

For a moment I was disappointed; with his broad white blaize and comical bay markings, he looked like a heavily built, sleepy circus pony. Christina suggested that he was very mature for his age, but Ted Dunne only said: "Lovely bone, 'e's got—make a show pony, if 'e was ridden properly—only a five-year-old."

It was a long walk across the field and I was glad that I was riding Symphony, who has a beautiful stride. Christina explained that I would be schooling Clown as well as herself and paid me several compliments, which I am not going to repeat. Ted Dunne looked at me a little dubiously and said I might be able to ride a bit, he dare say, and Symphony was a nice sort of pony.

When we reached the tree, Clown wakened from his day-dreaming with a start and galloped away down the hill, and watching his long easy strides, his beautiful carriage, I was disappointed no longer.

"Good pony, that—see what I mean?" said Ted Dunne.

"Yes," I said, enraptured; and then, at that very moment, something awful happened, which I think was entirely my fault. Carried away by enthusiasm for Clown, I had not been attending to Symphony and, as I spoke, she decided that she, too, would like to go down to the farm. With four bucks, which I will not pretend were large, she leapt into a gallop; the fourth buck left me sitting on the ground looking at her heels.

"Are you all right?" asked Christina.

"Oh, bother—yes, thank you," I laughed, springing to my feet and then, remembering Christina's remarks about my riding, I felt furious with myself. I had let her down horribly, just through pure inefficiency.

"Terribly stupid of me. I just wasn't attending," I said meekly.

"Well, we all 'its the ground sometimes, don't we?" said Ted Dunne in soothing accents.

"Do you think we will be able to catch Clown?" asked Christina.

"Drive 'im into the yard, I reckon," answered Ted Dunne, lighting a cigarette.

We walked across the field again, but when we reached the farm gate Symphony and Clown galloped back to the top.

"It doesn't look very hopeful," remarked Christina.

"I'll get old Charlie to lend us an 'and; wait 'ere a sec.," muttered Ted Dunne; and he climbed the gate, slowly and laboriously, and disappeared into a barn.

14

"Sorry I fell off," I said.

"You couldn't really help it. I'm sure I would have done the same—I mean it would have been different if you had been prepared," said Christina.

"He's a wonderful mover, isn't he?" I ventured—rather cautiously, because I have not "a good eye for a horse."

"Yes, beautiful, but I shouldn't think he would make a show pony. I don't know why, but I believe he'll just miss it."

"I thought he was too heavily built at first, didn't you?" I asked.

"Yes, he's certainly got plenty of substance and I like his deep girth. I should think he would stand up to a tremendous amount of work. Let's go up again and try to catch Symphony—she may have calmed down by now. You can ride Serenade if you like and I'll walk."

"No, thank you. It's my fault that I fell off and I'll walk," I said firmly.

It took us at least ten minutes to reach the ponies again and I grew very hot.

"I'm jolly glad that my parents don't own any fields this size," remarked Christina.

"It would be wonderful to gallop across, if it hadn't so many rabbit holes and ant-hills," I said, feeling in my pocket and producing a bit of bread, which I held out to Symphony.

"Come along, there's a good girl," I coaxed; but Symphony, who had been stabled during the last six months, did not feel inclined to exchange her freedom for a stale titbit. With a buck, she swung round and galloped all the way down to the farm again. Of course, Clown followed. They looked lovely with their manes and tails streaming, but we were too exasperated to admire them.

"I bet she's broken her reins. That bridle came from London—cost four pounds ten," muttered Christina.

"I'm terribly sorry; it's all my fault for falling off," I said unnecessarily.

I will not describe to you our feelings as we walked down after the ponies. Any one who has tried to catch an animal in a thirty or forty-acre field can guess the nature of them and those who have not will not gain anything from a description.

I took off my coat and carried it. The air had become hot and close. There would probably be thunder before nightfall. We were both silent. Then, when we reached the farm gate, we became hopeful—it was open.

"Perhaps they've caught them," suggested Christina.

Then Ted Dunne and an old farm-hand appeared.

"They're both in the barn. We tied your little mare up; 'er reins are broken and 'er saddle's slipped a bit," said Ted Dunne.

"Oh, Augusta! You *never* tighten your girths," muttered Christina. Aloud, she said: "Thank you very much. Did you drive them in?"

"That's right, miss—can't get 'old of Clown though. He's got wild-like—been turned out so long."

"Well," said Christina, "we don't really want to take him home to-day, do we, Augusta? We only came to look at him. We've got to get our parents' permission first. I'm sure they'll say 'yes,' but we must just ask them. What does he do exactly when he's ridden?"

"Oh, just plays up—excitable-like. 'E's never been ridden by any one good. Nothing bad in 'im."

Admiring Christina's tact, I stayed quiet, feeling that I had disgraced myself.

"He certainly looks very nice," she went on. "I suppose you would like us to have him until the end of October—ride him in the shows and then cub-hunt him?"

"That's what I was thinking of, miss."

We all went into the barn and gazed at Clown, as he cowered at the far end.

"Right, all being well, can we collect him to-morrow?" asked Christina in brisk and business-like tones.

"What about tack?" I said.

"Charlie, just pop along and find the saddle and bridle, will you?" said Ted Dunne.

The farm-hand shuffled away and returned a few moments later with an enormous rusty double bridle, with a roughened mouthpiece and long cheeks; and a cumbersome saddle, with knee-rolls and a very broad seat.

"On second thoughts, I think it would be less trouble if we used our own tack actually," said Christina.

"Take it back, Charlie," ordered Ted Dunne.

"Sorry to be a nuisance," I said. The old man shuffled off once more.

"Well, thank you very much—to-morrow then," Christina said, mounting.

Ten minutes later, we were on the road once more, riding between trees, with a roof of green leaves over our heads. I thought of Clown, seeing him as I had seen him—cowering at the end of the barn, miserable, frightened, pathetic. I wondered whether we were experienced enough to cope with him successfully, and then suddenly I was determined that we should succeed at all costs; suddenly I wanted to help him, to turn him into a well-schooled pony, not because he was beautiful but because I was sorry for him and wanted him to learn to enjoy his work. I never wanted him to look so miserable and frightened again.

Chapter 3 by Christina

FOUR DAYS LATER, on a wet and dreary Wednesday, Clown was installed in our only spare loose-box. Daddy had insisted that Augusta and I should not fetch him on the Sunday and had arranged for him to come by cattle truck, which certainly saved us a great deal of time and trouble, as we were to find out within a few days.

Solo took an instant dislike to Clown and, as the two loose-boxes were close together, he was able to vent his anger on the fat skewbald neck whenever it appeared over the door, which was at frequent intervals, because Clown was very excited and inclined to try to jump or climb out.

O'Neil was disapproving. To my surprise, Daddy had given us a set of lunging tackle and agreed that Augusta and I should look after our pupil by ourselves and that we could muck him out before breakfast during term; and I think Daddy's decision had offended O'Neil. When the cattle truck arrived and Clown was led out, O'Neil said: "Like a blooming circus pony," and hurried off—a bustling, disgruntled figure—to have lunch.

Mummy, however, admired Clown. She does not know much about ponies, but she liked his broad forehead and intelligent eyes, his rather high crest and gay markings; and she was annoyed by Solo's inhospitable behaviour. We stayed in the yard talking to the cattle truck driver for a while, before shutting Clown's top door and running in to lunch.

At two o'clock we started Clown's education. Following Augusta's sensible suggestion, we had decided not to ride him for several days. It was obviously silly to attempt to school him, while he was so petrified of us. We spent nearly the whole of that afternoon in his box; we taught him to eat out of our hands and to stand still while we ran our hands over his body. Afterwards we jumped my three ponies. Symphony showed enormous improvement and I began to feel quite hopeful about the Chilswood Show, although I knew that Daddy did not want me to enter her for the jumping class.

At two o'clock the next day we were again in Clown's stable, *and* the next day and the day after that. By Sunday we could put a head collar on him, pick up his feet and rub his ears, and we felt well pleased. "Slow but sure," said Augusta. But O'Neil thought we were feeble and over-cautious; he thought that we should be riding Clown by now; and it was partly his opinion that made us decide to lunge our new pony on Sunday.

With great difficulty we led him to the field, each holding one side of the head collar. He was very strong and nearly pulled us over, and Mummy—both my parents were watching—became quite alarmed with fear that he might tread on us. I was to try lunging him first, because I had had a little experience at the riding school where I had learned to ride. I took up my position in the middle, holding the rein in my right hand and the whip diagonally in my left, and Augusta started to lead him round. For a moment all was well; in fact, Daddy yelled *well done*; and then a second later, Clown shot into a gallop; I felt the rein curling round my legs; I held on and fell; and then the rein whizzed through my hands and dragged me for a few yards, before releasing my legs. I scrambled to my feet, with scraped fingers and palms, to see Clown galloping away across the field. Remembering our experiences at Beech Bottom Farm, I became pessimistic and wished that my parents were not on the scene.

"I'm terribly sorry. I just couldn't hold him," said Augusta. It was typical that she should be the one to apologise, although it was really no more her fault than mine.

"Darling, you *must* be careful—your *poor* hands," cried Mummy.

"That pony needs a man," said Daddy.

"Are you all right?" asked Augusta.

"Yes, thank you, quite all right," I said firmly, and the stars, which had been floating before my eyes during the last few moments, disappeared as I spoke.

"I'll try to catch him," said Augusta, with forced cheerfulness.

"I should have been more prepared. I believe anticipation is one of the keys to the art of riding. I don't think he needs a man, Daddy; Ted Dunne does not seem to have been very successful," I said, trying to hide my hands, as I followed Augusta.

We could not catch him; we could not even get near enough to tread on the end of the rein.

"You'll never catch that pony," said Daddy; and Mummy said: "Oh, do be careful, darling."

We fetched a bucket of oats, but with no avail—he would not look at it. Then, to make matters worse, Shannan appeared on the scene and started to chase him. I called Shannan to heel, but the harm was done, and now, instead of trotting, Clown galloped.

"You'll have to send him back," Daddy told us.

"Yes, darling," Mummy added.

I felt exasperated and, calling Augusta, retreated to the stableyard, where we sat on the white mounting block and tried to decide what to do.

The field gate opens on to the garden, and we usually lead the ponies down a cinder track behind the tennis courts. We did not think that we could drive Clown down this track, as Ted Dunne had driven him into the barn; there were too many borders for safety.

It was Augusta as usual who thought of a plan of action first. She suggested that we should use Solo to tempt Clown out of the field. Ponies are naturally gregarious animals and we agreed that, when our highly strung pupil had become calmer, he would feel lonely and probably follow readily enough.

I suggested that we might play a game of tennis, while waiting for him to reach this frame of mind, but Augusta said that she would rather read a book.

We tossed up to decide which way we would pass the time and, as I lost, we retired to a shady part of the garden with *Equitation* and *The Spirit of Man*.

An hour later, startled to action by the church clock chiming, we took Solo—we chose him because he never kicks—out into the field. Clown greeted us with rather hysterical whinnies, but would not come near. Presently we managed to lead Solo within six yards of him and then, leaving the gate open, we retreated with the little brown cob down the garden path. Reaching the tennis courts, we waited and soon we heard a whinny and then the scrunch of hoofs on the cinder. We paused for a moment before walking on; the scrunch of hoofs continued. We hastened across the stable yard and tied Solo to his manger, and, leaving the door of the loose-box open, hid ourselves. Only a few moments later Clown appeared, halted and stood stock-still, looking more like a statue than a real pony.

I wished that I had my camera with me, and Augusta apparently wished that she had a pencil and drawing-paper. Then he started to move and I felt a little nervous, because the stable yard is only separated from the garden by a low box hedge, and I could imagine Clown galloping over the borders. However, he walked towards Solo's box and my hopes rose. When he reached the door, Augusta and I rose with one accord; but we were too quick and, to our horror, only succeeded in frightening him down the drive towards the road. Too late, we realised how foolish we had been not to shut the gate, and then suddenly Shannan saved the situation. He had been straying in the road, and as Clown reached the bottom of the drive Shannan turned

21

up through the open gate and frightened him back to us. I yelled at Shannan to sit down, and for once he obeyed, so now the road was guarded, and in a crouching position, talking soothingly, I crept forward and took the end of the lunging rein.

Clown stood watching me and I tied it quickly round a tree, and then, holding out a handful of oats, Augusta approached him from the front. He snorted, trotted towards the garden and was pulled up with a jerk, and now he stood again, looked at us with startled eyes.

"One thing is definite," said Augusta, "we must spend more hours talking to him in the box before we try lunging a second time. He's obviously still terrified of us."

"The trouble is that the longer he stays in the box the fresher and nervier he becomes. It's difficult to know what to do, isn't it?" I said.

We waited a while before again approaching Clown. This time Augusta managed to take him by the head collar and we fed him on handfuls of oats for several minutes, before leading him firmly and gently into the loose-box. With sighs of relief, we shut the door. For an hour afterwards we played with him, picking up his feet, running our hands over his skewbald body, jumping up and down in front of him, waving our hands and banging them against our sides. We hoped this way to make him quieter. Both of us believed then, as we believe now, that too many horses and ponies are treated all their lives like nervous invalids. One hears children being told that they must not run past thoroughbreds, which seems wrong to us, because surely the one way to make a horse remain nervous for ever is never to allow him to become accustomed to sudden movement or noise. We had decided to treat Clown very differently from other young horses; we wanted him to become a thoroughly sensible pony.

At teatime we left him and assured Mummy that he was not vicious and had become much quieter during the last hour.

Chapter 4 by Augusta

THE NEXT WEEK passed rapidly and happily. Each day I rode Daybreak over to Hampton House and, on arriving, helped Christina to muck out Clown's box. At nine o'clock we went indoors and washed and started lessons with Madame Dupont, which lasted until half-past twelve, when we would break off for lunch. The afternoons we were able to devote to our ponies; in the evenings we had prep. to do, but not once that week was mine difficult; in fact each night it took considerably less time than was allowed and, when I had decided to do it with Christina at Hampton House, I was able to leave for home earlier than I had expected.

We did not lunge Clown again, deeming it better to wait until he was less nervous, but day by day, hour by hour, he seemed to become quieter; until he would hardly blink an eyelid when we put up umbrellas in his box, skipped or performed the most ridiculous physical jerks.

It was not until Sunday that anything happened to dull the merriment or disturb our peace of mind. Then, during the afternoon, when the sun was shining and the Carrs' green acres seemed wrapped in silence and calm, when the sky was as blue as English skies can be, and Christina and I were talking about bathing, Ted Dunne came to see Clown. When we confessed that we had not yet ridden his pony, he was bitterly disappointed, and I must say I felt a little ashamed. I was sure we were right, but at the same time I felt that we must strike him as a couple of cowards. I realised now that

Christina and I had never really considered falling off Clown; we had just thought it ridiculous to try to ride a pony who was so terrified of the human race. I tried to explain our methods to Ted Dunne, but, unimpressed by our loose-box tactics, we found it difficult to convince him. We pointed out that the last people who had tried to break Clown had, in all probability, failed through being in too much of a hurry. He said that he supposed we knew best and that he, for one, had never been able to stick on the pony for more than a few minutes. We showed him the other ponies and he admired Symphony and said that Daybreak was a useful sort, and then, after leaning against the saddle-room door for a quarter of an hour, he left and we stood in the yard feeling depressed.

"I do think we are right though," said Christina a little doubtfully.

"Let's saddle and bridle him," I suggested. It was the third time that Clown had worn Solo's tack, and we put it on without difficulty. Then, as he stood quietly and confidently, Christina put a little weight in the stirrups and we banged them against the saddle.

We both agreed that we would mount him in the loose-box first and, as he seemed so very sensible, we thought we might as well do it then and there. We tossed up to decide which of us should enjoy the honour and Christina won; so I held Crown while she quietly mounted and sat in the saddle, and then I led him round the loose-box twice.

"Perhaps Ted Dunne and O'Neil are right," I said, "and we have been too slow and cautious."

"They may be. I suppose time will show. I'll dismount now and get on the other side," said Christina.

She descended slowly and mounted from the right. Clown rolled his eyes and stiffened, but relaxed and looked happier after I had led him round again. Presently Christina dismounted and we made a great fuss of him. She and I felt very pleased now, so pleased

24

that we decided that we would try lunging him the next day.

I was to have first try this time, and I must say, on the following afternoon, as I stood in the field with the rein neatly coiled in my left hand and the whip held diagonally in my right, I felt a little dubious and very inexperienced. We had agreed that, because Christina had tried so unsuccessfully to lunge Clown to the right, I should attempt to lunge him to the left. Now, with the July sun shining in my face, I said "Walk on" quite loudly and very firmly.

Christina led him forward; the stirrups were crossed, but the saddle creaked and he laid back his ears nervously.

Since breaking Clown we have not used the leading method when lunging ponies for the first time; instead we have kept the rein very short and the whip pointing at their quarters, and have walked a small circle in the middle, so teaching them without a helper and firmly urging them forward with the voice and tactful movements of the whip.

But on this Monday I stood more or less still in the middle, while Christina led him by the bridle. He learned less than he would have learned the other way, because he attended to Christina instead of me, but on the other hand it was a safer method with a pony as nervous as Clown. After he had walked four circles to the left we stopped him, saying "whoa" in very long drawn-out tones. Then we turned him round and lunged him at the walk to the right, and there was no doubt that he preferred going round the other way. Now he became awkward and nearly pulled Christina over; with great effort she succeeded in keeping him calm and eventually he walked more sensibly, and we decided to take him back to his stable. It was with high hopes and a sense of achievement that we gave him his tea.

Next day we became even more hopeful. I rode Clown round the loose-box three times, and we lunged him for ten minutes in a saddle, bridle and cavesson, and the following day Christina rode him round the yard, with me at his head. By Sunday we could ride him up and down the drive—not being led but with one of us on foot walking just in front—lunge him at the trot to either hand, put an umbrella up within two yards of him, wave our arms in his face, hoot the car horn almost under his nose, pick up all his feet and tap them with a hammer.

We hoped that Ted Dunne would not come and see Clown, and our hopes were realised; Sunday passed without interference, and on Monday I led Christina round the field on Clown, and on Tuesday we took him to the forge. Christina walked with him and I rode Symphony, who was supposed to be a calming influence. After struggling for three hours, the farriers managed to put a set of shoes on him, and as we set off for home, Christina riding, I walking, we were happy in spite of bruises.

"Now," said Christina, "we can think about taking him out for proper hacks with the other ponies."

"Daybreak will be the best companion; he's so sensible," I said.

"Oh, I don't know—Serenade's pretty good," said Christina.

"As soon as Clown learns to behave reasonably well we might ride over and see Piers and Tilly. I've never been to their place, but they don't live far from here, do they?" I asked.

"About eight miles, I think. I've never been there either. Piers told us that they had a little cottage in the middle of a wood, with a yew tree clipped in the shape of a peacock outside the front door—sounds fascinating; but do you think they will want to see us?"

Piers and Tilly are two children who belong to the same riding club as Christina and me. We met Piers at the club camp, and Tilly, his younger sister, later during a club expedition to London. They own a little

26

grey mare called Seaspray, a wire-haired terrier called Bandit and a pair of bantams.

"I don't think we would be a nuisance—not if we rang up first. I expect they would like to see Clown. I know if *they* had a new pony I should love to see it," I said. And I imagined a round, pink cottage with a thatched roof and tiny windows, and remembered Piers —tall and fair in jodhpurs—and Tilly—dark and pretty, with a fringe and very blue eyes.

"Whoa, steady—don't be silly. That's all right, Symphony . . ." Christina quietened her mount, who was setting a thoroughly bad example by shying at every dustbin, and, as it was "dustbin day," there were rows of them.

It started to rain slowly in big drops. We met a woman with an umbrella, and when Clown passed her without hesitation we realised that we had not tried our patience in vain. Foxey Lane gave us shelter and we whistled gaily as we walked down between its wet banks, which were white and fragrant with the last of the meadowsweet. Nearing Hampton House, we saw an old bent man approaching from the other direction, and even when we were at least fifty yards away, we could tell that his attention was riveted on Clown. Reaching us, he said:

"Excuse me, miss, but that b'aint young Ted Dunne's pony, is it?"

"Yes, he is, actually. We've had him for about a fortnight and are rebreaking him," I answered, watching the man's expression of mild curiosity turn to one of dismay.

"*Not* Ted Dunne's?—can't be—what 'ad so many off? Yet 'is markings are the same, right enough— patch on the cheek and all." He spoke more as though he was talking to himself than to us.

"I think the pony's the same—called Clown. But how does he get his riders off? What does he do which is so terrible?" asked Christina.

27

"You've done wonders, wonders," mumbled the old man.

"Please don't speak too soon; we've hardly ridden him and he reared enough in the forge this afternoon," I said.

"Ah, *Clown*—that's what they used to call 'im," the old man continued to talk as though to himself. "And *rearing*, 'e was always one for that—came down on young Smallbone's leg once—'ad to go to 'orspital. Ah, you'll know it, young ladies, you'll know it before you've finished."

Suddenly the old man became quite vehement. Looking me straight in the face with his blue eyes, he asked: "And 'ow much is Ted paying you for this breaking?—if I might be so curious as to inquire."

Somehow "inquire" sounded odd, spoken by our new acquaintance.

"Nothing at all; we are doing it for fun," replied Christina firmly.

"*Fun*," he laughed, "you'll 'ave plenty of that; so young Ted's getting it done for nothing, is 'e—always was a bit of a smart one, Ted was. Well, good luck to you." The old man stumped away, leaving us strangely silent with our thoughts. And grim thoughts they were too.

I was the first to speak. "Gosh, it does look as though we are in for it. We mustn't let Clown come down on *our* legs. I never have liked rearers and Mummy can't bear them, so we had better keep quiet about that old man."

"He was probably a little insane. I shouldn't take a lot of notice of what he said. It's no good jumping our fences before we meet them. Clown hasn't stood up much yet, has he? Except in the forge to-day, which was most likely due to nerves. It'll be rather fun if we make him into a perfectly schooled pony and then find that he was supposed to be unbreakable." Christina was reassuring and I found her optimism infectious. "Perhaps we'll be able to ride him on Bank

Holiday. We'll have to pull his mane—it's quite un-plaitable at present, and I say, won't there be a lot of him to wash. You'll have to do most of him, because I've got Daybreak and he's always a job."

"Perhaps, perhaps," echoed Christina, and then she started to whistle—a melody from *Bitter Sweet*.

I was silent, because I cannot whistle or sing in tune. I thought of the future and of Clown's part in it; gradually the rain stopped falling and the sun came out, and the air smelt of glad, wet grass and wild summer flowers.

Chapter 5 by Christina

ALL TOO SOON Clown gave a demonstration of rearing; in fact when we took him out for his first ride. On this fateful day the sun was once again shining, shining with the golden warmth of July and unaccompanied by any sense of stuffiness. Augusta and I were feeling optimistic; the ponies were looking lovely, clean and well groomed. Madame Dupont had been in a good temper that morning, and even though one of the subjects had been geometry our lessons had seemed easier than usual. Augusta had been marked ten out of ten for both her history and English, and we could for once look forward to our evening's prep. without worry. And now it was one of those afternoons when it is almost impossible not to feel gay, when everything around one seems filled with the joy of life. A light breeze stirred the beech leaves, little clouds darted cheerfully across the blue sky; the ripening corn rustled pleasantly and the birds, wood-pigeons and thrushes, cooed or sang from the thick green hedges. We had started before two, and at first we met a few workmen returning from lunch, who remarked agreeably on the beautiful weather.

Augusta had recently acquired a book about the painter, Cezanne, and—ardent supporters of the Impressionist school—we discussed the pictures reproduced in this book, at least really Augusta, who knows more about Art than myself, put forward her ideas on the subject. She was in one of her more talkative moods, whereas I felt inclined to be silent, so we got on very well together.

As we left Foxey Lane Augusta said: "By the way, have you seen the book Mummy gave me about Rodin? It hasn't many plates, but it's most awfully interesting." And then the trouble began. As she spoke, I felt Clown hesitate and used my legs without any result. Slowly and firmly he laid back his ears and stopped.

"What's the matter?" asked Augusta, turning round to see why I hadn't answered her question.

"I've no idea. Come along, *there's* a good fellow. Walk on," I said.

"I'll go first. Perhaps he's frightened," said Augusta, urging Daybreak into a trot.

She rode forward several yards, but still my mount stood his ground. I dismounted and tried to lead him, without success; he did not look frightened, but merely sullen and obstinate.

"I think that I had better be firm, right from the start," I suggesting, remounting.

"Okay," said Augusta.

I put the reins into one hand, used my legs vigorously, but without any response, and then, grasping my stick firmly, hit him once—only once; for the next moment he was standing on his hindlegs, rearing and pawing the air.

"Lean forward, you idiot," I muttered to myself, slipping my hands up the skewbald neck and grabbing the mane; then we came down to earth again and Clown was standing still once more.

"Gosh! well stuck on. What *is* the matter with him? I'll ride on a bit farther. He surely can't want to be left alone." She almost disappeared round the corner, but Clown stood his ground. I hesitated, patted the hard sleek shoulder, squeezed with my calves, kicked with my heels and then summoned my courage and hit him just behind my left leg, saying: "Walk on," loudly and firmly.

Again he reared, staying balanced on his hindlegs

for what seemed like an age, before coming down to earth again.

"This is terrible," said Augusta, returning. "I'll try leading him, shall I?"

"Righto," I answered. She took hold of his bridle and saying "Walk on," tried in vain to urge him forward. I felt my heart sinking, my courage ebbing away. Was he really an incurably vicious pony?

"He doesn't seem frightened. He's not peeping at anything," I said.

"It's just sheer stubbornness; you can tell that by his expression. He's a jibber," added Augusta.

"I might try turning him round and round, so fast that he can't rear, hitting him at the same time," I suggested, thinking: Well, if he does fall over backwards, I'll probably land clear—no reason why I shouldn't.

"Let's try coaxing a bit first. We may be wrong; he may be terribly afraid of something that we can't see or something he can smell. The other day I got quite cross with Daybreak, because he wouldn't approach a walled farmyard. At last, with alternate calming and scolding, I succeeded in getting him through the gate to find to my horror that they were just starting to burn a pig, which Daybreak, of course, had smelt yards away."

"All right, I'll try," I said. "Come along, Clown; there's nothing there, nothing at all. It's quite okay. Walk on—there's a good fellow."

My efforts were in vain, so again I dismounted and tried leading him. He walked forward a few steps this time and I became hopeful, but a moment later he stopped and refused to move in any direction, until I hit him—then he reared, right up, pawing the air and nearly hitting me with his hoofs.

"Careful," warned Augusta, dismounting too.

"I say, he does look sullen," she went on. "I hope he's not incurable."

"Of course he isn't—we are going to cure him," I said firmly.

"Yes, we certainly are," said Augusta, as though she spoke aloud in an attempt to convince herself.

"I think I had better be severe," I said, remounting.

"Right, I'll walk on a tiny bit."

Again I mustered my courage; then, filled with determination, I used my legs vigorously and tried to turn Clown round in circles to the left—the idea being that, if I turned him round fast enough, he would not be able to rear and would eventually tire of this treatment and admit defeat. The plan failed. He knew too little about the "Aids" and too much about the art of rearing. I turned him round once before he stood up again. I wished I was a better rider, as I grabbed the mane, and then a terrible thing happened—Mummy appeared in the car, on her way to change the library book.

"Gosh, that's put the cork in the bottle," exclaimed Augusta, seeing the familiar bonnet come slowly round the corner.

Clown came down on to his fore feet again, and Mummy stopped the car. "Darling, what *are* you doing? That pony must go—he's dangerous. Get off now, *quickly.*"

The sun seemed to lose its golden radiance, the sky to turn a greyer hue; as she spoke, the birds ceased their song and the earlier enchantment left the day, leaving only an uninspiring air of usuality. "That pony must go," I thought, dismounting slowly, and, standing upon the hard road, I felt bitterly disappointed.

"And how many times has he done that terrible rearing?" Mummy's voice came to me.

"Only a few," said Augusta.

"A few's enough. You must lead him back home, darling, really you must. What Daddy would say if he saw you, I don't know."

I glanced at Mummy to make sure that she was

33

A terrible thing happened

serious. She looked very cool, calm and collected in a linen coat and skirt and smart high-heeled sandals.

"Righto," I said. "I'm most awfully sorry if we gave you a fright."

"Oh no, we can't give in," cried Augusta.

"It was horrible, darling, coming round that corner and seeing you in the air, perched precariously on a rearing horse. I was terrified that he would fall over backwards."

"Oh, Mummy, I wasn't 'perched precariously.' I was quite firm," I said indignantly.

"I was just going to suggest that I should ride Clown. Not because I imagine that I'm better than Christina; but because I don't see why she should have all the difficult work nor take all the risk," said Augusta.

"I don't see why either of you should risk anything for Ted Dunne—certainly not your necks. Come along now, lead that pony home. Hurry or you'll be late for tea and have no time for prep.," said Mummy.

"It's awful to accept defeat. I mean, he'll be much worse to-morrow—probably won't leave the yard. Can't I have a try on him, please, Mrs. Carr?" asked Augusta.

"Really, I think if your mother had been here and had seen that pony rear she would say *no* most firmly," said Mummy, and Augusta, knowing that this was true, dismounted and said: "You ride Daybreak, please, Christina, and I'll do the leading then."

"Are you sure you don't mind?" I asked.

"Certain. Here you are. Hop on, for goodness' sake." She handed me the pony's reins and took Clown.

The journey home was almost irritatingly uneventful and proved, all too clearly, that Ted Dunne's pony was a nappy and confirmed rearer. He jogged confidently beside Augusta, never hesitating or shying, perfectly aware that he had just won a triumph and obviously looking forward to his tea.

"What are we going to do?" asked Augusta, leading him up our drive.

"We can't take him back; it would be too feeble;" although we must think of our parents' nerves," I said.

"I think he's just absolutely stubborn through and through. He certainly doesn't seem frightened of us any more. You know yesterday he bit my coat buttons and seized my pocket," said Augusta, shutting the loose-box door.

"That's because we've petted him too much—fed him out of our hands too often. O'Neil's right," I said, silently reproaching myself.

"Yes, it seems that when it comes to jibbing it would be better if he was more frightened of us. Rather surprising that he isn't very obstinate on the lunge rein. I wonder what started the rearing business. He must have done quite a lot of it with Ted Dunne. Sore mouth perhaps or tender feet, or something," mused Augusta.

"Let's read some of my books and see what they say on the matter," I suggested.

"Okay, and finish Clown off after tea—do his box and everything. He's got some hay and water at present," said Augusta.

Half-way down the path, before reaching the house, we turned and gazed at the beautiful skewbald head watching us intently over the loose-box door. There was nothing which could denote stubbornness or a mean temperament about its shape, nor in its expression at this moment. The eyes, set wide apart, were large and generous, the cheek broad and cleanly cut, the nose fine and tapering and the ears small and neat. The general impression it gave was one of intelligence, gaiety and kindness. We looked and looked again and then turned, of one accord, sadly and silently towards the house.

Chapter 6 by Augusta

CHRISTINA'S BOOKS were neither consoling nor helpful; the two more modern ones told us that rearing was undoubtedly the worst vice, being both dangerous and incurable; while those written in a more vicious and less enlightened age differed; some suggesting that the horse that twice reared should never be trusted again, others that the animal should be pulled over backwards—either mounted, when the rider must be careful to roll clear, or on long reins—or that a bottle should be broken over the culprit's head, or that he should be burned on the gaskins and under the tail with a red-hot iron.

"Not very helpful," said Christina, sitting on the table. "It looks as though Clown really is incurable."

"I wonder what started him rearing—a too tight curb-chain, a sore mouth perhaps or just round and hasty handling. That was a murderous bit of Ted Dunne's, wasn't it?" I said, seeing again the large rusty bridle, the long cheeks and roughened mouthpiece.

"We must remember that all is not yet lost. He's only had one rearing fit and he hasn't even tried to get into a stance while being ridden round the field nor going to the forge. He may have just succeeded once with Ted Dunne and recalled the triumph for the first time to-day," said Christina.

"If that is so, we must have done immeasurable harm this afternoon; if it was just an experiment on his part, it proved a mighty successful one. I say let's leave these pessimistic books and go and feed him. I must start for home soon. I've got to clean out the

37

duck-house and feed Lucifer. I can't leave Mummy all the work to do," I said, picturing my mother pushing a heavy wheelbarrow across the orchard and my dog sitting on the white doorstep, watching forlornly for my return.

We went outside. Filling up Clown's water bucket, Christina shouted: "I've had a brain-wave. Why not ring up Eleanor and ask her advice? One of the objects of the club is to help and advise its members."

"Jolly good idea," I answered. "I'll take the water bucket if you want to do it now."

"Oh, I don't know about that. You're a much more tactful person than I am and I'm sure you get on better with Eleanor—she thinks I'm rich and spoilt."

"Oh, she *doesn't*. She thinks you can ride. Look how well you managed Swallow at the camp gymkhana. As for me, I maddened everybody the whole time by losing my belongings and leaving grooming tools in Daybreak's stall. Besides you're much better at explaining things to do with horses; you know all the right terms. I always make a muddle."

"Nonsense, you don't."

"Well, let's toss up."

"Okay."

"Got any money?"

"Sorry, Christina, not a sou."

"I'll pop indoors and get some."

She disappeared into the house and I stood looking at Clown, admiring his long sloping shoulders, his long thighs and forearms, short cannon bones and round hard feet, admiring, too, his strong quarters and well let down hocks. It's a pity that he should be wasted, be considered incurable, I thought. He's the type to jump, but of course you can never be sure; there are hundreds of ponies with beautiful conformation with every reason to jump, who never turn into anything— partly bad schooling, sometimes lack of courage, I suppose.

"Heads or tails?" yelled Christina from a window. "Mummy's tossing."

"Tails."

There was a moment's pause before Christina yelled: "You've won. Do you want me to ring up?"

"Please—I'll saddle Daybreak."

As I girthed up my pony I thought about Eleanor, who had arranged the riding club camp the year before. I remembered how well she rode, how competent and yet polished she looked on a horse, and I remembered her well mannered dark brown gelding, Harkaway. Surely she could help us?

Christina opened the window again.

"Eleanor's gone away to Italy," she yelled. "Won't be back for a fortnight."

"Oh gosh! What a beastly shame—I mean for *us*. I was just piling such high hopes on her advice. What are we going to do? Any more suggestions?" I asked.

"Find someone else to help us."

"Who—Mrs. Nailer?"

"Oh *no*, not her," Christina recoiled at the mere mention.

"Well, she does know what she's talking about," I said.

"Yes, but she doesn't like me. Don't you remember what a fool I was at the club rally?"

I *did* remember now. Christina had made some tactless remark, while being instructed by Mrs. Nailer, and had been turned out of the class. A beastly thing to happen to any one, I thought, and said: "Who can you suggest?"

"What about Philip Lockheed? He breaks in a lot of horses very successfully—or so it seems—and was very agreeable when we looked round his place."

"He'll think us an awful nuisance," I said.

"Yes, I suppose he will; it's not as though we know him very well."

"Rather cheek of us, I think."

"Perhaps you are right. I expect he's very busy and

39

it would be an awful bother for him to have two tiresome children pestering him for advice. I suppose we had better forgo the idea. I'll come down and help you with Clown," said Christina dismally, shutting the window.

I bridled Daybreak and then wandered out into the yard. The sun had left the sky and an early chill seemed to have descended on the Carrs' garden. Dark clouds hovered ominously behind the chimney pots of the house, and the birds, which usually sang with such abandonment from the tall beeches, were silent. Presently Clown's head appeared over his loose-box door and a feeling of helplessness assailed me.

What a tragedy it seemed that no one could speak horse language, that no one could explain to him that he must learn to earn his keep or be destroyed. He watched me with full, shining brown eyes, with an intelligent expression which filled me with sadness. Somehow I felt certain that if we failed Ted Dunne would end Clown's life, and it seemed terrible that a young healthy animal should die through a misunderstanding, without knowing the reason or that he could save himself.

I heard Christina's footstep on the path.

"We must cure him somehow. We can't let him go for dog's meat. It would be a crime—murder; it's unthinkable," I said.

"Perhaps Ted Dunne will send him to someone more capable than ourselves. There's no reason to be so sure that he will be destroyed," said Christina calmly.

"But it's so feeble just to take him back," I argued.

"Well, we mustn't wreck our parents' nerves. Dash it all, Mummy's right—a rearer *is* dangerous."

"Listen," I said, gripping the loose-box door. "He's only reared to-day; we don't know that he's a confirmed rearer. Let's ride him in secret then. I know it would be deceitful, but it would save our parents anxiety and perhaps Clown from destruction."

"I've just been talking to Mummy; she says that

40

either we get some knowledgeable person to help us or Clown goes back."

"Oh, Christina, I don't believe you care," I said with vehemence.

"Of course I care," she answered, sitting down on the mounting block. "I'm only trying to be firm and sensible. It's no good getting worked up. We've got to think of our parents, Clown, and *lastly* our pride."

"You do sound virtuous," I said, almost laughing, although in my heart I was despairing.

O'Neil came round at that moment to take a last look at Symphony, Serenade and Solo. He's a brisk little man, but a horsy snob—preferring a disagreeable show horse to a sweet-tempered but inferior animal—and I have never felt that he liked either Christina or myself much. To-day I said: "Hallo, we're just going to finish Clown off for the night; he hasn't behaved too well this afternoon, I'm afraid. Daybreak's made one of the boxes dirty, but I'll clean it out before I go home."

O'Neil paused for a moment, looking me up and down, as though noting that my jodhs were badly cut and my shirt old and darned. Then he said: "Oh, that young 'un—you pet him too much. You don't want to give him so many of those lumps of sugar," and proceeded to deliver a short and sensible lecture on the folly of over-petting horses, particularly young geldings or colts; a lecture which I think we both took to heart.

"Well," said Christina eventually, "Clown reared to-day—right up. How do you think we can stop that?"

"Get be'ind him with a whip, give him a good hiding," answered O'Neil, with such assurance that we felt he must be right. Christina looked at me and I looked at Christina, and then she said:

"Could you help us to-morrow, do you think? Please, Mr. O'Neil."

The groom was silent for just long enough to let us know that he was thinking things over carefully, possibly remembering that we had not deigned to ask his advice earlier. Then he told us that he would with

Riding Daybreak home in the cool calm of the evening

pleasure and that he was not frightened of rearers and had mastered many a vicious brute in his time. His tone of voice, the words he used made me feel a little apprehensive, but at that moment any assistance seemed better than none; his offer gave me food for hope. It's always darkest before dawn, I thought, and "Not by eastern windows only, when daylight comes, comes in the light."

"Thank you very much indeed. After lunch—okay. Yes, Augusta will be riding him, I suppose. It's your turn, isn't it?" she turned to me.

For a few seconds I saw myself astride Clown, clinging to his mane; then suddenly I became filled with determination. To-morrow was to be a day of triumph. Thanks to my magnificent riding, our pupil would be cured; by nightfall he would be a different pony, ready to learn all that we could teach him.

"That's right, my turn," I answered. And then O'Neil went into the forage-room and we fed Clown. And it wasn't until I was riding Daybreak home in the cool calm of the evening, that I began to wonder whether I could sit a rear; and it wasn't until I saw the chimney pots of our dear white house that I imagined myself falling off in front of O'Neil, spoiling Clown and wrecking our parents' nerves.

Chapter 7 by Christina

AUGUSTA TELLS ME that, riding Daybreak over to my
place the following morning, she was filled with mis-
givings. I certainly felt dubious, especially during
breakfast when Mummy questioned me on our plans
for Clown. I told her that O'Neil would be helping us
and that he was fairly confident that he could cure him
of rearing without endangering ourselves. I was very
vague, but Mummy seemed satisfied; in fact much more
satisfied than I was myself. Whenever I recalled
O'Neil's "Get be'ind him with a whip. Give him a good
hiding," I became apprehensive and wished in a way
that it was I who would be riding Clown, for, although
Augusta is more tactful and has a more natural-looking
seat than myself, she seems to fall off more often, and
I sometimes think it is better to go to hospital oneself
than to watch a friend go. I regretted now that I had
been persuaded from ringing up Philip Lockheed.

Neither of us could attend to lessons much that
morning and Madame Dupont became impatient, and
made grimaces of despair and called us both "lazy-
bones," which, pronounced angrily with a French
accent, sounded rather funny. I don't know which of
us, governess or pupils, was the most relieved when
the nursery clock's hands reached half-past twelve.
I'm sure all of us had been watching them more intently than usual. Lunch was late—a rare occurrence
at Hampton House, but somehow on this day we
expected the unfamiliar to happen. I'm afraid we
gobbled and spoke little, for our thoughts were on
Clown and we could only look forward to two o'clock.

Mummy was very decent and allowed us to go out directly lunch was over, and we were in Clown's box as the church clock struck. O'Neil helped us with the saddling and bridling; he was in an excellent temper and walked about with the righteous air of one who, having been misjudged and unappreciated for years, has at last been recognised for what he is worth, has proved in the end that he was right from the very beginning. Even his expression seemed to say "I told you so."

Augusta mounted in the schooling field. I stood at Clown's head, while O'Neil hovered in the background with a whip in his hand.

"I'll just lead him round a few times so that he can settle down. Perhaps he won't rear at all to-day," I said hopefully. Augusta fiddled with her stirrups for a moment, before saying: "All set."

We walked round the field twice and then I released my hold on the bridle and went in front of Clown, who, apart from looking nervous, behaved beautifully—just followed me as meek as milk. Augusta whistled (it's a habit of hers, I notice, to whistle when she's riding a difficult young horse) and O'Neil stood by the gate, still with the whip in his hand. I was glad that we were not by the road, for although I know there are some horses and ponies which do need and deserve a little rough treatment, I did not want any strangers to see us at work to-day. I was not so sure whether the whip was the right cure for Clown, and anyway I hate to see ponies being hit at any time, and I felt horribly guilty.

Soon I ran and Clown trotted, and then I joined O'Neil and left Augusta to walk round without me. O'Neil said that it did not look as though he was needed, and I, on tenterhooks, told him not to speak too soon. I watched the rider and pony change the rein, and more intently as they came past the gate, where Clown hesitated, rolled his nearest eye towards us and then went straight by. I sighed with relief. If Augusta had had trouble and, with O'Neil's help, fallen off, I should have been haunted by remorse, because it was I who had suggested that we should enlist the groom's assistance. I felt now that I understood why schoolmistresses are so fussy; it must be awful to be responsible for other people's children. Of course I wasn't responsible for Augusta, but I could not forget that it was I who had taken on the schooling of Clown.

"I shouldn't ride him round too many times or he'll rear out of sheer boredom," I suggested, and my words irritated my companion, who said, probably quite rightly, that we had got to have the fight sometime.

"Wouldn't it be better if we postponed it until he understood the aids more?" I asked, but was given no answer. A few moments later it started to rain—really hard—and Clown put his head down and tucked his chin in towards his chest, and went sideways. He looked so miserable that we decided to end the lesson and hurried back to the stables. Cleaning tack, we discussed his behaviour with O'Neil, who laughingly said that it was his presence that had frightened the pony into good conduct.

Later, at tea, we heard that Mummy had been watching Augusta riding from the window, and was very pleased and reassured by what she had seen. It seemed ridiculous now that only twenty-four hours ago we had been so downcast, fantastic that we should have thought of sending Clown back untrained to Ted Dunne, impossible that we had imagined that any one might have considered destroying such a promising young pony.

Augusta said that when she reached home she was going to open a bottle of cider and play the gramophone to celebrate Clown's better behaviour. I said that Clown was going to be one of the best ponies that had ever looked through a bridle, and Mummy said we had better be careful and remember that "Pride comes before a fall." While eating éclairs, we decided to ride Clown to see Piers and Tilly in about four days' time, when most of the schools would have broken up. We also decided that we would exercise him on the lunge rein and from the saddle in the field, and not venture down Foxey Lane on the following day.

And then the very next afternoon everything seemed to go wrong again. Clown reared by the gate and O'Neil hit him across the hocks with a whip, and then he leaped forward, tried to break through the hedge and fell down on his knees. I sat up his neck, and Mummy shrieked from the garden that I was to dismount at once. I scrambled back into the saddle, and Clown dragged himself out of the hedge and stood still trembling, while Augusta took hold of his bridle. Then, O'Neil, to our surprise, hit him across the gaskins and this sent him careering across the field. I had lost a stirrup and, glad to be away from the gate, I made no attempt to check him.

We reached the far end in no time and swerved left; I retrieved my stirrup, sat down in the saddle, braced my shoulders and pulled him up, noticing that as he halted he dropped his nose and relaxed his jaw. He eyed O'Neil nervously and breathed heavily.

"I say, can't he go? He's got a wonderful gallop," I yelled.

"Christina, darling—do be careful," called Mummy.

"Well, that made him move, didn't it?" said O'Neil with satisfaction.

"I don't like him standing up on end. It's so dangerous," said Mummy.

"Supposing, Mrs. Carr, I go and fetch Serenade and ride him round with Clown? There won't be any rearing then. Is that okay, Christina?" asked Augusta.

"Quite—good idea. I'll dismount for a few moments."

On the ground, I said: "Well, he didn't rear right up to-day. You couldn't call that one by the gate more than a half. Honestly, Mummy, I think he'll be all right now."

Augusta came back very quickly, and with Clown

following Serenade, we schooled in the field for a while, mostly at the walk with occasional halts.

O'Neil returned to the stables and all went well until Clown noticed this; then he began to look and edge towards the gate again.

"He *is* nappy," said Augusta.

"I think he'll be perfectly all right if we keep over this side of the field and keep moving," I told her, and squeezed with my outside leg. I have always been taught that, when riding, you should look in the direction you wish to go, and now, with exaggerated care, I gazed away from the gate, away from the house towards the far hedge, which I think was the reason for me not seeing Shannan. Why Augusta did not hear or see him, I do not know, unless it was because she was deep in thought. She *is* one of those often irritating people who become so immersed in their thoughts, as to be almost entirely unaware of what is happening around them. In fact sometimes on these occasions you have to speak to her two or three times before she really hears you. Anyway, I don't think either of us were to blame for what happened, although I shouldn't have fallen off. One minute I was looking towards the tall green hedge and the next I was slipping sideways; Clown was turning, twisting, galloping, and then I landed on the ground with a soft thud, heard Augusta say "Whoa, steady," and saw Clown's skewbald quarters and white tail, and a few seconds later Shannan was licking my face and Mummy was running across the field, saying: "I knew this would happen."

"Why did he do that?" I asked.

"Your blinking dog came tearing towards him looking like a wolf. Are you all right?" said Augusta.

"Quite, thank you. Sorry, Mummy; it was stupid of me to come off, but it wasn't really Clown's fault. Shannan, have you *no* common sense?" I jumped to my feet. "There was nothing vicious about that shy," I added.

48

The next minute I was slipping sideways

"I don't like that pony, and unless you get someone competent to help you, he must go, and I mean it."

"Yes," I said, and "Have you anything to catch him with—piece of bread or some oats, Augusta?"

"No, sorry. Oh yes—here we are—two lumps of sugar."

"Can I have one, please?"

"Certainly."

With a sinking heart, I approached Clown, a lump of sugar in my outstretched palm. He watched me, walked away and then stood still, again eyeing my every movement. Slowly, quietly, I came up to him and took the rein, before he ate the sugar.

"Well, at least he's become easier to catch," I said. "I had better ride round once before he goes in. I mean, it's not good for him to stop directly someone falls off."

"Oh, darling, I would rather you didn't, really I would," said Mummy.

"Shall I have a try? I'm used to falling off, so if anything does happen I'm not likely to hurt myself," suggested Augusta.

"No," said Mummy, "no, certainly not. I won't be responsible for you."

I could see she was firm. "I think we ought to lunge him for a few minutes then," I said.

"I'll fetch the tackle. Come on, Serenade," called Augusta, riding out of the field.

"What a good thing you were wearing a hard hat," remarked Mummy, looking at the small dent in my bowler.

O'Neil came back and watched us lunge Clown. He said that I had been silly coming off so easily, and that Shannan was disobedient. I agreed with him and sat on the gate and admired Clown's impressive action and superb carriage. His head seemed higher and his balance more perfect than they had seemed last week. While living in the stable his figure had improved, and now I suddenly noticed that he possessed a gracefulness which we had not recognised before. He looked like a circus pony, but like a beautifully trained and well-bred circus pony. Now that he was thinner, his appearance could not possibly be described as comical and his markings no longer struck one as grotesque. I could see him placed first in a showing class. I could see him performing high school, I could see him jumping enormous fences.

I felt very moved and very sad, and vowed secretly that we would not return Clown to Ted Dunne.

"I think he's had enough now, don't you?" said Augusta, calling the pony in to her. I agreed, and slowly, deep in thought, we returned Clown to his box.

Chapter 8 by Augusta

"WE'LL *have* to ring up Philip Lockheed," said Christina, as we jogged down the drive on Symphony and Solo, half an hour later. "It's that or sending Clown back."

"I wish I knew him better," I said, remembering that I had upset a cup of tea in his house.

"Surely, if he's fond of horses and interested in riding, he won't mind giving us advice. I mean, we needn't ask for him to come and help us or anything —just tell him we are in a fix—Eleanor's away, etc., etc."

"Yes, it sounds easy," I said.

We cantered along a track which ran beside a golden cornfield and led us at last out of the sun into the coolest of beech woods. Solo's stride seemed short after Daybreak's, and his ears seemed incredibly near my mouth. He is a very compact cob, short everywhere, and noticing this once again, I decided that it was not surprising that he had dislodged so many riders, for there was really nothing to keep them on, no long sloping shoulders, no firm length of neck; you had only to slip a little way to be off altogether.

Christina was still thinking about Philip Lockheed. "I don't suppose he would really mind. He and his wife were very agreeable when we looked round their place," she said.

"Well, will you do the ringing up?" I asked hopefully, "because I'm sure to say the wrong thing; you know how tactless I am."

"Nonsense," said Christina sharply, "you know you are renowned for your humble approach."

"Let's toss up again when we get home—it's the fairest way," I suggested, annoyed by my companion's last remark.

"Righto—bet I'm unlucky," said Christina, and she *was*. She called tails and the battered penny, tossed by Walters, fell heads uppermost.

"What did I say! I should think I had better ring up after five o'clock. People are generally in reasonable tempers when they've had their tea, and I shall certainly feel stronger when I've had mine."

"Thanks awfully, Mr. Walters. It's strange for me to be lucky. Yes, I think five o'clock will be a most tactful time," I said.

Mr. Carr was home that afternoon and at tea he asked for a report on Clown's behaviour. Christina was marvellous; she put on a bright expression, talked in a sensible and confident tone of voice, dwelling for a long time on the pony's improved carriage and balance, and only just mentioning his *little rear* and her *unalarming toss*. But Mr. Carr was sceptical.

"Your mother tells me a rather different story," he said, "and I'm not sure it wouldn't be better to send the brute back to its owner without further ado. Hang it all, Christina, I've bought you the three best animals I could find—there's not many in England can beat them at their job, as has been proved—I don't see why you must risk your neck with someone else's common cast-off."

I disliked his swankiness, but I could see his point of view. Christina had other ideas, which I could also understand.

"But, Daddy, these well-trained ponies—they're just the point. I want to be able to ride unschooled ones as well. I want to learn to break them in. I don't want to go through life unable to ride anything which has cost under three figures."

"You needn't worry about your riding, darling; look how well you managed Phyllis what's-her-name's very ordinary pony," said Mrs. Carr.

"Oh, Swallow; he had obviously been well schooled once and had got spoilt. There was nothing in riding him," Christina told her.

"We are going to get someone to help us with Clown now, if that's okay, so I think we may have less trouble in future," I ventured.

"You said O'Neil was going to make such a big difference, but the pony reared again yesterday and bolted with Christina," remarked Mrs. Carr.

"Only a half-rear—nothing dangerous—and he didn't *bolt*, Mummy, he was frightened by the sudden and tactless appearance of Shannan and *took hold* and galloped a few yards," explained Christina.

"Well, I've spent close on two hundred pounds on your riding lessons, and if at the end of it you can't sit a pony galloping a *few yards* you ought to be utterly ashamed and are obviously not fit to break-in any animal, let alone a brute which is known to be difficult." Mr. Carr spoke more sharply than I had ever heard him speak before. A silence followed his words. I wanted to support Christina, but could think of nothing to say. I felt small, untidy and incompetent. Why should any one be interested in my opinions? I asked myself, and the longer the silence lasted, the more difficult it became to speak. Then suddenly, for no reason at all except that I was trying to take a sip of tea and thinking of something else, I upset my cup. The contents splashed all over the carpet—we were in the drawing-room to-day on account of Mr. Carr being at home.

"Gosh, I *am* sorry," I exclaimed in horror, leaping to my feet. And thinking: you stupid, clumsy little idiot.

"Sit down," said Mrs. Carr wearily. "Walters will mop it up." She rang the bell and I guessed that she was thinking: What a tiresome awkward girl she is, always knocking over something. I shall be glad when the holidays start and she's not here so often. Actually, it was the first time that I had upset anything during meals in their house, but I felt very angry with myself. I apologised to the butler, who mopped with effective and expert speed. When he had left, the conversation returned to Clown.

"Who are you getting to help you this time?" asked Mrs. Carr.

"Philip Lockheed," replied Christina.

"Never heard of him," said Mr. Carr.

"Oh, Daddy! You *must* have. He show jumps and shows. He's got three stallions, and Gay Truant, the arab, has won almost everywhere. He was champion at Islington, and his son Gay Courtier did well as a show hunter last season. Don't you remember Macaroni and Spaghetti, two big cream horses, jumping at Tidhampton?"

"Yes, I believe I do. But can he teach you anything? Dash it all, you win quite a lot yourself." Mr. Carr looked, with pride, at the latest of Christina's cups, which had been allowed the honour of residing in the drawing-room, and Christina, who does truly, I believe, dislike talking about her winnings, almost snapped: "Of course he can. He breaks and trains all his own youngsters and has tons of experience. Anyway, it's five o'clock now and I must go and ring him up. I hope to goodness he won't think it cheek."

"Don't be silly, darling, he can't possibly think it's cheek. You've been to his place; he's interested in riding; it's not as though you're a complete beginner; he ought to be only too pleased to help you," said Mrs. Carr, but Christina was already out of the room.

"May I get down? I think I had better saddle Daybreak," I said.

"I love the way you say 'get down.' Did you have a high chair for a very long time?" asked Mrs. Carr.

"I don't know; I don't think so. Mummy always says it too—you can get down now, Augusta—so it sounds quite natural to us," I said, rising to my feet. "Thank you for the lovely tea—sorry about the cup."

"That's all right. Don't worry your head about it. Good-bye," said Mrs. Carr.

I wandered out into the hall. Shannan was there. I knelt down and talked to him. He was lying on a priceless Persian rug, which he nearly covered with his huge grey body, and gazing with amber eyes across the sweep of gravel towards the road. Outside it started to rain again in big round drops. I should get wet before I reached home and that would mean changing.

"Oh dear, I must go. I wish I had brought a mac," I said to Shannan, and then Christina shouted from her room—she has a smart white telephone at her bedside: "It's all right. He's offered to come over to-morrow afternoon. Isn't it wonderful. I'll come out and help you with Daybreak and tell you the rest of the conversation."

"Hurray," I called. "Come on, Shannan."

Together, the dog and I, we ran to the stables.

Tightening my girths, Christina said: "He was most awfully affable, gave me quite a surprise. I started off by explaining who I was—at least where I lived and how I had seen his place—and then I told him that we had a difficult pony to re-break and were making rather a mess of things and wondered whether he could possibly give us a little advice; and he asked what the trouble was and, when I explained, he said he thought it would really be best if he came and saw the pony. I said wasn't that an awful nuisance? and he said no, not at all; it would be a pleasure."

"Gosh, that's marvellous. Did he put forward any views over the telephone? I mean did he say, dear, dear, that sounds bad or anything?" I asked.

"Well, he seemed to think the rearing was rather serious, but he wasn't pessimistic and he didn't say we had been utterly stupid. Can I ride along with you on Serenade? He must have some more exercise, and if I clean the tack afterwards O'Neil won't really mind."

"What about your prep.?" I asked, mounting.

"I shall get up early and finish what I don't do to-

56

night. I shall be so excited about Clown to-morrow that I'm sure to wake at dawn," replied Christina.

"You'll get wet," I told her, but she only said: "Never mind."

So only during the last half of the way home was I alone—or rather without human companionship, for you cannot be described as "alone" when you are astride that most inspiring and kindest of animals, the horse!

I went down a bridle path, instead of through the usual woods, where the ripening corn, the green hedges and the little haystacks standing in the corner of distant fields, and the old magnificent trees, conspired to make the landscape look like a Constable painting. It had stopped raining now, and the earth smelt warm and fresh. Daybreak's coat steamed and he smelt, as wet grey horses do, like a leghorn hen. I started to sing and I sang until I reached home, when Mummy came running out of the house to ask after Clown. Patting Lucifer, who clawed my legs and cried with pleasure caused by my return, I told her all, explaining that to-morrow would see a changed pony, that Philip Lockheed would know how to deal with him. Mummy, who, like Mrs. Carr, is fussy about hard hats, said that I must remember to wear my crash cap and that I mustn't do anything silly, and that hard men to hounds like Philip Lockheed, who had no children, didn't think broken bones mattered but she did and that, quite apart from her nerves, I might consider the doctor's bill before I did anything rash. I said, yes, I certainly would, and then we went indoors to prepare supper.

We ate scrambled eggs on toast, and raspberries and cream that night, and I dreamt that Philip Lockheed didn't advise us about Clown, but said that he had come to teach us how to drink tea, and that all the cups of tea I upset would go on the doctor's bill, so I had better be careful or my parents would be bankrupt.

Chapter 9 by Christina

AFTER LUNCH the next day, we dashed out to the stables and groomed Clown a second time, because we wanted the Lockheeds to be impressed by his appearance.

It was another pleasant afternoon, with a light refreshing breeze, occasional sunshine and a patchy sky of fluffy white and clear blue.

Philip Lockheed and his wife arrived soon after two in a Ford brake, accompanied by a pretty golden cocker spaniel and Laird, their white West Highland terrier, both of which they left shut in the car. We all shook hands very formally and Mrs. Lockheed admired Shannan, who skipped and frolicked round us in sudden, mad ecstasy. Then we wandered from loose-box to loose-box, looking at Symphony, Serenade and Solo and talking to O'Neil, before eventually reaching Clown, who, seeing so many people advancing, dashed into his farthest corner and stayed there—a miserable, cowering pony.

"Oh, he's skewbald," said Mrs. Lockheed, apparently surprised.

"Quite a nice sort—got a good front and an intelligent type of head, too," remarked her husband. "Is he always so nervous? Do you know how he's bred?"

"We thought he might be part Arab," I said.

"Yes, quite likely. His mane and tail, and broad cheek and fine tapering nose give one that impression. Don't you think so, Antonia?" he addressed his wife, who agreed and added that the almost complete absence of fetlock pointed to the same fact also.

Augusta said: "Would you like to see him lunged first? I mean before we ride him."

58

"Yes, please; that would be grand. Christina—it is Christina, isn't it?—says he goes very well now."

"Well, we think he does, but you, of course, may find that he's bending his head the wrong way or not flexing his ribs or something," suggested pessimistic Augusta, disappearing into the saddle-room.

Walking out to the schooling field, we discussed the Lockheeds' stud. We were told about their latest foals and we learned that Marksman, a promising young horse, which we had seen lunged when the riding club went to their place, had been sold. I remembered their whitewashed stables, so neat and picturesque, warm, thatched and homely, and hoped that one day I might own such a yard.

We had tossed up before lunch and arranged thus that Augusta should ride Clown and I lunge him.

As I took hold of the head collar and led him into the middle of the field, I heard Augusta telling the Lockheeds about the trouble we had had at the end of Foxey Lane. I sent Clown round to the left first, and within a few minutes was called to halt and was told that I was too stationary, that I should move a little myself so that I could keep just behind my pupil.

"It's especially important with a pony which is inclined to jib or stop," explained Philip Lockheed. "It's fatal to get your whip ahead of them; if they suddenly swing round you are powerless, whereas if you've got yourself properly placed, just the pointing of the whip or a neat flick will do the trick. You see, you must make a triangle of your horse, the rein and whip as the two sides, and yourself the apex."

"Is there anything we can do to stop a horse pulling us over?" asked Augusta.

"Well, once he starts to go you obviously can't hold him; you're not nearly strong enough. The point is that you shouldn't let a horse find that out, never give him a chance to want to tear around. These troubles generally begin because the breaker has been in too much of a hurry, asks a horse to trot before he understands what it's all about, or to canter before he's sufficiently balanced or supple. Of course there are some which are more devilish than others, and some which like their little bit of fun and get away from you without really intending to—if you see what I mean. Actually, you will find that youngsters are far more likely to misbehave or play the fool in a biggish field like this than in a smaller, enclosed space, where there's nowhere for them to go if they do get loose. Next time your parents are feeling rich and affable, you might tactfully suggest that they could fence round a portion of field, approximately one hundred and eighty feet by sixty feet, as a school for you. Later, of course, when you are earning some money or have an allowance or your parents are again feeling rich, you ought to construct a surface for the school, which means: rubble and fine clinker ashes, and tan and sawdust. Everything's much easier then. You can ride in all weathers and, if you put up a few markers, you can see that you do the school figures—such as diagonal changes of hand, half voltes and the usual balancing exercises, not to mention half passes, with precision. It's marvellous, if you've got a proper surface, after rain, too, or if you are energetic enough to rake the tan, because then all your hoofmarks are new and you can see whether your horse has been going straight and whether your circles are true circles."

"Yes, it sounds wonderful, but my parents are not at all rich, Christina's might do it, of course," said Augusta.

"You had better be careful, Philip, or, before you know where you are, you'll have hordes of angry parents after you," said Mrs. Lockheed, laughing. Then she added: "Clown certainly goes well on the lunge rein," and, at the same moment I, who had not heard the conversation but had it repeated to me afterwards, called him into the middle, patted the warm skewbald neck and sent him round the other way. He behaved beautifully, and I must say I felt rather pleased as

I led him up to the onlookers a few minutes later. Mrs. and Philip Lockheed tried to pat him and said things like: "Well done," and "That's fine," but he ran away from them and hid behind me, because he was still frightened of adults, especially men.

Then Mummy appeared and I introduced her to the Lockheeds, and she said. "Oh, I shall be *so* glad if you can give them some good advice. Christina, of course, can *ride*. I've heard people say that she is the best child rider in the country." (Here I should like to add that the man who made that rash statement knew practically nothing about horses or equitation.) "But I'm absolutely terrified sometimes when I see that pony rearing and Christina perched on top. It is so kind of you, and I do hope you'll be able to stay and have some tea."

"It's very nice of you to ask us, but I'm afraid we have to be back home by four," said Mrs. Lockheed.

Mummy and the Lockheeds talked to each other, while Augusta and I saddled and bridled Clown.

"Right," said Philip Lockheed when we were ready. "I'm glad to see that you ride him in a rubber snaffle. Don't you think that, as his jibbing and your difficulties occurred in the road, it would be just as well if we took him there first?"

"Okay," said Augusta, putting on her crash cap.

"Be careful," warned Mummy.

"Bring the lunge rein, head collar and whip, Christina, please," said Philip Lockheed.

Augusta mounted, slowly and correctly.

"I see you are like Philip and get on facing the head," remarked Mrs. Lockheed.

"Antonia and I have never been able to agree on the mounting point," explained Philip Lockheed. "I say that our way is best, because: if the horse moves you are hopping forwards instead of backwards; if you are mounting a tall horse you are not so likely to stick your toe into his stomach when facing the head, because you can put your foot parallel to his shoulder;

when training youngsters it is easier to teach them to stand to be mounted when facing the head, because, while holding the reins in your left hand you can, with the help of a longish stick or whip, prevent him from swinging his quarters away with your right hand."

"Yes, *and* get cow-kicked," said Mrs. Lockheed.

"Not at all; when facing the head we can watch his ears and eyes and thus know when he is about to kick or bite us; whereas you, with your attention glued on the heels, get a nice juicy bite and jump swearing into the middle of next week," contradicted Philip Lockheed.

"I don't, because I keep the horse's head turned away from me."

"And get his quarters bumping into you."

They both laughed. "It's no good," said Mrs. Lockheed. "We'll *never* agree on that, so we might as well give up arguing."

We reached the bottom of the drive and turned out into the road.

"Clown's certainly got a nice long stride, which means a good gallop, and he carries himself well too —a useful type of pony," said Philip Lockheed.

A few moments later trouble began. Clown's head went up a couple of inches, he stared up Foxey Lane, as though there was a monster at the end waiting to spring on him, and then he stopped dead and swung round on his hocks. Augusta turned him back, so that he was facing the same way as he had been before, and he stood stock-still.

"Say 'walk on' loudly and firmly and use your legs," said Philip Lockheed.

She did as she was bade, without effect.

"Can you try leading him, Christina?" he asked.

I put down the whip and rein and head collar, and took hold of Clown's bridle. "Come along. Walk on; there's a good fellow," I said. The pony chucked up his head, gazed with goggling eyes down Foxey Lane and remained standing. Augusta used her legs vigorously, and then suddenly he gave a half-rear and swung round again, pulling me after him. I turned him back and tried once more, but this time he reared considerably higher.

"Obviously that's no good. Now, Augusta, hop off and put the head collar and lunge rein on him and take the whip and drive him calmly down the lane. Christina, you mustn't help. If possible, it is best for the rider to do this by himself."

"I don't wonder your mother is alarmed. These rearers are the very devil, sometimes," remarked Mrs. Lockheed.

"Well, he's only gone up really high once," I said, "and it just happened that Mummy appeared on the scene at precisely that moment."

"That's a comforting thought, because, as no doubt you know, a confirmed rearer is incurable ninety-nine times out of a hundred," said Mrs. Lockheed.

Augusta was driving Clown down the lane, He stopped and tried to turn round, but with a neat flick on his flank she sent him on again. After they had walked about fifty yards, Philip Lockheed told her to bring Clown back and, when she had returned, to mount and try to ride down the lane again, holding the lunge rein in a neat coil. She tried, but in vain. Clown reared and immediately she was told to dismount and resort to lunging once more, which order she obeyed successfully. This was repeated four times, and then, the fifth time, Augusta managed to make him advance from the saddle, which we hailed as a triumph. Now, we all walked for about half a mile and then branched off down a track, which runs round in a small circle and passes one of our field gates. In this track Clown jibbed, but, after being lunged for some distance, gave in, when brought back to the spot where he had stopped, and allowed himself to be ridden the rest of the way home without further trouble.

Back in the stable yard, Philip Lockheed kindly

gave us some good advice. He suggested that, for the next few weeks we should mostly hack Clown, up and down hills and over uneven ground, to build up his muscles and balance him. He told us to put a head collar under the bridle and to take a lunge rein and, if possible, a whip, so that we could dismount and drive Clown on when he jibbed. He said that it was important that the rider should do the lunging and that, each time, Clown should finally be ridden over the spot where he had jibbed, so that we had in no way given in. He told Augusta that she did not keep her knees close enough to the saddle and that, with patience and careful handling, Clown might become quite a useful sort of pony.

Mummy, a tall, slender figure, came out from the house and thanked the Lockheeds for their kindness, and said were they absolutely sure that they could not stay to tea? Mrs. Lockheed said yes, unfortunately they were certain that they could not; and Philip Lockheed said that he had been very pleased to help us and that he hoped he had been of some use, and that he thought we had a reasonable chance of curing Clown, because he thought we might have just got the pony in time. He was of the opinion that Clown had only tried it on once or twice during his life and had then been turned out to rest in a field by a rather scared and very ignorant Ted Dunne. The cause, in the first place, had probably been some frightening object— a cart-wheel in a hedge, a dustbin, something of that sort—most likely the pony had stopped to look and then received rough handling, several jabs in the mouth with the severe bit I had described and a lot of unwarranted stick. He hoped that Mummy would not see either of us perched on a rearing pony again and said that, should we get into more difficulties, he would be delighted if we would give him a ring. Of course, if Clown continued to misbehave, the kennels was the only place for him—there was no doubt about that.

Augusta said: "It would be a tragedy to destroy one so young." And then the Lockheeds got into their car and, after we had thanked them again, left.

Mummy said: "Well, remember, darling, any more trouble and that pony goes straight to the hounds," and went indoors, and Augusta and I loitered in the yard talking to O'Neil, before adding hay to Clown's net, cleaning his tack and finally going in to tea.

Chapter 10 by Augusta

I AM NOT going to describe fully the four days which
followed that of the Lockheeds' visit. On the first we
brought O'Neil a birthday present—a packet of
cigarettes and a brown and white spotted tie—otherwise
we continued our education with little enthusiasm and
our riding with considerably more enthusiasm, and
hacked Clown, quarrelled with Clown and triumphed
over Clown. Now, thinking back, I especially remember one hot afternoon when we tried to ride him to
Bumpers to see Mummy; how we struggled with him
at some cross-roads when the heat was so stifling that
we longed to fling ourselves down into the tall grass
and meadowsweet, growing before the bank, to gaze
upwards to the sapphire sky, or longed to reach the
river and plunge into the cool dark waters and come
out calm and refreshed; how we drove him up and
down that dusty road, and tried again and again to
ride him, how the buses repeatedly groaned past at
the most awkward moments, how an agreeable, deaf
farm labourer tried to help us, and how, at last, Clown
gave way and I rode him by the signpost and on to
Bumpers.

But it is the fifth day that I shall never forget. Term
had ended, and when I wakened I had that wonderful
feeling of relief and freedom that one experiences on
the first day of the holidays.

During the previous evening, Christina and I had
arranged that we should ride over this morning to see
Piers and Tilly—at least start in the morning and
arrive at their cottage in the afternoon—and the

thought of this expedition made me feel yet more cheerful, and I whistled incessantly as I helped Mummy with the washing up. It was Martha's day off. I had several jobs to do in the house, and as a result did not arrive at Christina's place until nearly half-past eleven and she was annoyed at my lateness, because she had had to muck out and groom Clown all by herself. I pointed out that she did not have to: (a) make her sandwiches or bed; (b) help her mother wash up; (c) feed hens, ducks and bantams; (d) ride two miles. My points were received in silence and it would have been all right if I had stopped then and there. But I had not; instead I added that Christina was unobliging and groom-ridden, and it was the last insult that cut deep; for if there is one thing of which she is afraid, it is that she is thought too superior to, or incapable of, attending to her own ponies. Seeing her expression, I regretted my insinuation as soon as it had passed my lips, but, not being a nice child, I could not bring myself to admit that it was unjust. And so at twelve o'clock we left Hampton House, with two packets of sandwiches each, a flask of water and all the usual lunging tackle, in deadly silence. I was riding Solo, as arranged the evening before, and he was very fresh; he jogged and sidled, and shyed at every opportunity in the most ill-mannered way. Now and then, Christina glanced with a frown in my direction and I guessed that she was angry, because I was setting a bad example. I decided that Solo needed more exercise and less oats, and wished that I was a better rider. When we left Foxey Lane we were assailed by horse flies, which sent Solo, who has a docked tail, into a frenzy. He kicked and stamped, snorted, trembled and swung his head round to knock them off his back and flank. I picked a beech twig, with which to beat them off, but my attempts did not meet with much success and we continued to set Clown a bad example. Soon we turned down a little path, between two cottages, where the tall bracken brushed against our feet and swarms of ordinary flies arrived, as if from thin air, to reinforce the others and plague our mounts and ourselves. We had never before explored this path, and having found it on the map marked as a bridle road, we had expected it to be considerably broader. Each moment, now, we hoped it might improve, but we hoped in vain. The bracken grew taller; the branches above our heads became lower and rabbit holes lay hidden on either side.

"This is awful," shouted Christina, breaking, at last, our long silence.

"I should think Solo will go mad in a minute. Poor fellow—the flies are just eating him," I replied, lying on his neck to avoid the branches and putting one leg forward against his shoulder to avoid a tree-trunk.

"It looked so nice on the map. I thought we would be able to canter some of the way or at least trot. We'll never get there in time now. I don't think Solo will go mad, but mind out, he may buck," warned Christina.

And then suddenly the bracken cleared and was replaced by brambles and nettles, and nut trees and hawthorns; and here the path petered out altogether. The next twenty minutes were terrible and unforgettable. Now, if at any time I am cross, bored or dissatisfied with my lot in life, I recall them and thank Fate that I need not enter that ill-favoured wood again, and immediately a feeling of relief replaces that of discontentment; but that day I was not to know that the experience would do me any good and, as I saw Clown misbehaving with Christina and tried to calm the lathered Solo, I cursed my bad luck and stupidity.

Of course, when the path petered out we should have turned back, but, obstinate and annoyed, we scorned to be defeated by mere scrub and undergrowth—as Christina described it. I think that, with Serenade and Daybreak, we might have won through. Clown and Solo, however, were very far from being suitable mounts for such an expedition, and we had only plunged a few yards when Clown stopped and said plainly that he could go no farther.

At the same moment, Solo caught his hindleg in a fallen branch and, being a very nervous pony, panicked. He ran backwards, bucked and nearly dragged me off under a bough. When I managed to regain control and look around, I saw Clown giving half-rears, with a tree either side and a tree behind him. If Christina comes off, she'll hit her head on a trunk, I thought, and, if she stays on, she'll crack her skull on a branch.

"I should dismount," I called, hastily jumping from Solo.

There was not nearly enough room for us to use the lunge rein, so we tried to lead Clown, which, although he followed, was miserable work. Both ponies loathed the undergrowth and, where it was high, stopped until we could persuade them to jump. I tore the sleeve of my shirt—it was rather a nice blue poplin one—and Christina scratched her face. At last we found a little path and our hopes rose, but they were doomed to disappointment, for a few moments later an enormous tree lay across our way; a tree which we could climb, but the ponies could not jump, because of overhanging branches. With difficulty, we turned round and retraced our footsteps, until it was possible to re-enter the wilderness of brambles and nettles, and struggle once more amongst stunted, ivy-twined trees.

Clown had jumped on to Christina's ankle and she was limping, and then, to make matters worse, I tore off the sole of my shoe, which was infuriating, but really my own fault because I had insisted on wearing my oldest pair, because they were the most comfortable. I expect it might have been all right if the sole had come clean away, but it did not. Somehow, it managed to leave several nails behind, which pricked my foot. They were very tiresome, and presently I said that I must ride. Christina decided that she would do the same, and we mounted in a little hollow. We had now lost all sense of direction, as well as all hope of arriving at Piers' and Tilly's cottage by half-past two. Silently, because all our attention was needed for the guarding of our faces and knees from scratches, scrapes and bangs and the guiding of our mounts, we plunged forward. There were less flies here, and the air was heavy with the musty smell of ivy and wood and old dirty earth. Only occasionally could we see a patch of sky, and from this dim interior it looked grey and dismal. Solo became suddenly bored and started to trip over roots, but Clown followed more sensibly. Then suddenly we saw light ahead, and I gave a yell of hope. As we advanced, the way became easier; there were less brambles and the trees grew farther apart and we saw a few wild anemonies, and a moment later we saw a thatched roof and a high, green thorn hedge, and suddenly we realised that we were back where we had started.

It was an infuriating discovery, and we both exclaimed loudly with annoyance and surprise at the predicament it presented. Which way now were we to go? Neither of us felt inclined to enter the wood again, and by road it was a long call to Piers' and Tilly's home.

I was the first to think of another plan. I suggested that we should ride down the road—it led eventually to London—in the opposite direction to Hampton House, looking carefully for a telephone in the hope that we could ring up our friends to apologise and ask them if they knew the shortest and best way to their cottage; and also look for signposts mentioning Wayward Hollow, which was our friends' address.

Christina agreed to this suggestion, but, although we rode on and on for what seemed like an age, and although it was a busy main road, we saw no telephone kiosk and no signpost mentioning Wayward Hollow. Cars whizzed by and occasionally a bus or a charabanc, and now and again a lorry, and there were a few bicycles, but it was the lunch hour and we met no friendly farm labourer or country person to tell us the way.

At last, in exasperation we turned down a quiet lane, hoping that we might find a cottager in his garden who might help us.

"I don't know why we didn't bring the map with us or at least we might have looked up an alternative way before leaving home. It would have been a much more practicable thing to do," I said regretfully.

"Let's stop and have lunch. I know we've been jolly stupid and I need some bread and cheese to keep my spirits up," said Christina, "but I'm glad we didn't bring the map; it would have ruined the shape of our pockets and made an awful line in our coats. I know I'm only wearing my third best one, but I don't want it to get disreputable." She dismounted and took a package out of her beautiful leather sandwich case. I jumped off and dragged my dingy packet of sandwiches from my pocket. We allowed the ponies to graze while we ate, but Clown did not give Christina much peace; he wanted her lunch, and when she had finished that he wanted the flask of water. Solo behaved beautifully, so half-way we swopped and I held Clown while Christina lay for a while in the long cool grass at the side of the lane.

The food and water certainly revived our spirits and we felt much more cheerful as we mounted and continued our journey.

"At least we are exploring new ways," remarked Christina.

"At least this expedition is good for Clown," I added. And soon we forgot that we were late and admired the countryside, which was truly picturesque. I do not believe that I have ever since seen so many charming little cottages or pretty gardens in one afternoon. They lay hidden behind thorn hedges or looked down on us from tall flowered banks or clustered gossiping around village greens or peered over dark ponds. They stood amid flowers with meadows and fields of ripening corn before them, and woods rising steeply to meet the hot clear sky as a background. They peered through a screen of trees or clung upon hillsides or lay, snug and warm in sheltered valleys. There were cream cottages, pink cottages, white cottages, mossy-brick cottages, timbered and plastered cottages, and cottages so shrouded by creepers that you knew not of what they were built. There were thatched roofs and tiled or slate roofs; there were stone roofs and, here and there, horror of horrors, a corrugated iron roof. We loved them all that afternoon; we wanted to live in each one. We forgot the inconvenience of small rooms, the dirtiness of oil-lamps, the danger of claustrophobia. And we forgot that Christina was riding a young pony, until, suddenly, he stopped, stopped dead and swung round on his hocks. It was a goat that he had seen—a strangely meek-looking goat with lop ears—a goat which Christina and I recognised at once.

"Skiddaw!" we cried, and "Gosh!" and "Hallo! my friend. Fancy seeing you."

And then, out of the wonderful, symmetrical, Queen Anne house walked Nigel, yellow-haired, pale-faced, spectacled, with the same elderly, pompous air as I had noticed when I first saw him at the riding club camp nearly a year ago.

"Good heavens! This is indeed a surprise—Christina and Augusta. Do you often venture in this direction?" he inquired. (Inquired is the only verb which will do.)

"Hallo, we are lost. We are trying to find Piers and Tilly," I explained.

"Lost? You do not look very alarmed by your plight. Are you following in Bertram Mills's footsteps —I mean, why the circus pony?"

"He's nothing to do with a circus. Up to date he's a failure," said Christina.

"Like so many of us," murmured Nigel sadly.

"What we would like to know is the way to Piers'

72

and Tilly's cottage. We were supposed to be there by half-past two. Do you know it?" asked Christina.

"Know it? Good heavens, yes. It's most uncivilised, hardly in contact with the outside world; suitable for a refuge; you could go there to meditate awhile—*Solitude and Want, twin nurses of the soul*—you know what I mean, don't you? But to live! Goodness, I wouldn't live there if I was paid."

"It's all very well to stand here quoting, but can you tell us how to get to this terrible spot?" asked Christina, glancing at her watch.

"Not possibly. You know how useless I am about the way. I couldn't explain to save my life, but I could show you the way or, at any rate, Punch could. If you like to wait a moment, I will have him saddled and bridled in a jiffy."

"Oh, that's wonderful. Thank you so much," I said gratefully, imagining that our difficulties were now at an end.

He went and Christina said: "It's not so wonderful as you think. He'll be hours. Don't you remember how he always held every one up at the camp?"

"Perhaps he's become quicker with age. Let's ride on as far as his front gate, anyway."

My suggestion proved to be easier said than done. We had forgotten Nigel's goat, Skiddaw, but Clown had not. He had no intention of approaching her; he seemed to think that she was highly dangerous, although a meeker-looking goat I do not think you could find anywhere; and she made matters worse by clanking her chain. There was no doubt that he was really frightened this time, that he was not jibbing out of pure stubbornness. Even the lunging rein and whip did not work their usual wonders. Christina did not want to make a fool of herself in front of Nigel, but there was no escape for her. Clown was still the wrong side of the gate when he returned with Punch.

"Good heavens!" exclaimed Nigel. "I *said* that

73

Even the lunging rein and whip did not work their usual wonders

skewbald was a circus pony and I believe I was right. Just *look* at him rearing."

"He's *not* a circus pony and never has been a circus pony. Do you think you could possibly move Skiddaw, please, Nigel?" asked Christina, clinging on to Clown, whose only desire was to gallop away in the opposite direction as fast as his legs would carry him.

"Of course, certainly—a pleasure. Augusta, would you be so good as to hold Punch a moment?" said Nigel, dismounting with a grunt, like an old gentleman.

When the goat was moved, Clown became calmer and at last we were able to coax him by the gate, Nigel rejoined us and we proceeded at a brisk trot along the verge of the road. We were not so late as I had imagined; the time was only a quarter to three and, according to Nigel, we had just over a mile to go. Christina was a little worried about Clown's behaviour; she was afraid that we had given in to him, that he would now jib whenever he saw a goat. But Nigel calmed her by suggesting that we should ride over to his place for tea in a day or two and turn Clown out in the field with Skiddaw; an invitation which we accepted gladly. Presently, breaking into a walk, we talked about the other club members, and I learned for the first time that Phyllis had probably failed in the school certificate and that the Folley twins had been chosen to represent the country in a junior hockey team this winter. Nigel talked a good deal, more than either of us. Personally, I like him. I know that he is sarcastic, that he is a very poor athlete and inclined to seem proper; but I also know that he can be very amusing, that he is sarcastic about himself as well as about other people, that he appreciates art and literature, is a good conversationalist and, in spite of a rather sceptical outlook, very kind-hearted.

Christina likes Nigel, because, she says, he was nice to her at the riding club camp when the Folleys and Charlie Dewhurst were beastly; but she thinks that he is affected and slow and often tedious, that he is odd, too—rather a laughable character. This is probably true, but I believe that it is better to be a laughable character than to be dim and hardly distinguishable from your fellow-men. After all, there is not nearly enough mirth in the world, and if, intentionally or unintentionally, you cause a little, you have done a good deed.

To-day, thanks to Nigel, both Christina and I were giggling when, at long last, we saw our friends' cottage through the brown-grey trunks of the beech trees.

"Oh, it's lovely," I cried. And it *was* sweet—not a horrible baby pink, but a wonderful musky old pink; not neat and smart like a doll's house or a Dutch cottage, but shabby and romantic; not creeper-entwined, but with a few white and yellow roses, hanging in cascades close by the door. In the little garden, which was just lawn and a few brave flowers, grew a dark yew tree, clipped in the shape of a peacock; in the little shady paddock was a loose-box with a door, which matched the colour of the beech leaves, and over it looked the dear grey head of Seaspray, our friends' good grey mare.

"Coo-oo! Here at last," I called.

Bandit, Piers' dog, began to bark, and Tilly's bantams cackled shrilly.

"I believe no one is at home, after all," said Christina.

Chapter 11 by Christina

WE DID NOT STAY long in Wayward Hollow, because when we remembered that we had a far ride to home there seemed little time to spare. We rang up our parents and explained that we would be late for tea, and then Piers and Tilly kindly invited us to turn the ponies out in the paddock for a while. We hoped that they would eat and rest; but they galloped madly up and down by the hedge, only stopping occasionally to squeal and speak to Seaspray. Piers and Tilly both admired Clown, but Nigel tried to irritate me by muttering "circus pony" and "produce of Bertram Mills" at annoyingly regular intervals. Piers said that, as we were not staying to tea, we might as well have some chocolate, so we wandered into the cottage which, although pretty from the outside, was obviously small and inconvenient inside. Augusta, so much better on these occasions than myself, took an interest in the checked table-cloths, the rush-chairs and the Impressionist reproductions, and soon Piers offered to show us round the whole cottage. Although only sixteen, he is tall for his age, and he had to bend his head as he went through the stair door and led the way up the steep and narrow staircase.

There were three bedrooms, all absolute tiny, and Piers and Tilly used theirs as sitting-rooms as well, which struck me as rather a difficult arrangement. I liked Tilly's best; it was very sweet and gay and rather untidy, with a divan bed with a frilled chintz cover, and a white dressing-table almost completely occupied by china horses; the cream walls were lavishly decorated by post-cards—dark horses ploughing against an orange sunset, a herd of ponies galloping over a hill, manes and tails flying, a hunting scene, an old English sheepdog—those were a few of them, the ones I can remember most easily. The ceiling was very low. Sitting up in bed, Tilly must have been able to touch it; and the eaves came right down to reach the floor. But the window was the most fascinating thing about the room; it was minute and, looking out across the paddock to the wood's cool greens, you could rest your hands on the tiles of the cottage roof. Tilly showed us her horsy scrap-book, and then we looked at Piers' room, which was slightly larger and had a yellow bed with a checked cover that matched the curtains, rush-mats and a yellow rush-chair, which reminded Augusta of Van Gogh's well-known picture—she had seen it lately in the Tate Gallery—and a plain deal table which, Piers assured us, he scrubbed regularly once a fortnight. The walls were distempered a rather yellowy cream, and the two pictures were, to my mind, definitely garish. We peeped into Piers' and Tilly's parents' room, which was furnished in oak and had two windows, before going downstairs and enjoying what Tilly called a "chocolate feast," which meant that we each tried to make a tuppenny bar of Nestlé's chocolate last as long as possible. Bandit, Piers' wire-haired terrier, hearing the rustling of paper, appeared on the scene and ate a few chips and cleared up the crumbs. I told our friends how we had been lost in the woods and how lucky we had been to come across Nigel's house, which we had never seen, and then, as they were curious about Clown, I related his history to date. Nigel said we would never cure such a well-trained circus pony, and Piers said rearing was a nasty vice, the worst in his opinion; but Tilly was optimistic and said no animal with such an intelligent and agreeable head as Clown's could possibly become vicious, except through a misunderstanding, and she betted we would soon cure him completely. Although she was only twelve and not a very experienced rider, her words cheered and heartened me, and, as I caught Clown, who seemed to have become much more friendly during the last few days, I bet Nigel sixpence that we *would* cure the so-called circus pony completely and that this arduous task would be finished within six months. Nigel took me on, saying that he supposed there was nothing wrong in me wanting to lose sixpence.

Piers said that Seaspray had not been exercised to-day and, if we didn't mind, he would like to accompany us half-way home and show us a short cut, which was the most wonderful bridle path ever known. We, of course, said that would be fine, and a few minutes later the four of us rode away from the pink cottage into the woods.

Augusta said she was sorry for poor Tilly having to stay behind, and Piers explained that after these holidays he would never ride Seaspray again, because he would be too heavy; in fact he would hardly ever be able to get any riding at all until he earned his own living, because his parents could not afford to buy a bigger mount unless they sold Seaspray, and Piers and Tilly were determined to keep their pony until she died or had to be put down.

Looking at the little dappled grey mare and remembering how well she had behaved at the camp, I sympathised with them.

"So," Piers went on, "I'm going to ride her mostly this half, and afterwards Tilly, who doesn't look as though she will grow very big, will have her for ever and ever." He patted the short grey neck, and Seaspray cocked back one dappled ear and broke into a jog trot.

When Augusta and I were alone again, walking down Piers' grassy, sun-kissed track, we agreed that we must hold a party, a wonderful long party with ice-creams and meringues, éclairs and trifles; a party which started at two and went on until nine.

"We don't know half the club members nearly well enough," I said. "In the town where I lived before we came to Hampton House, there used to be billions of parties—too many really."

"What I always feel about parties is that they don't go on long enough; you've just begun to settle down and become accustomed to your fellow-guests, when you find it's time to go home," said Augusta.

"Well, if ours goes on till nine, every one should have time to know every one else," I said.

We decided then to invite at least fifteen children, including Augusta's cousins, Barbara, Stephen and Jill, and to hold the party at Hampton House, because if it was held at Bumpers Mrs. Thornedyke and Augusta would have to do a mass of extra housework.

"I think we ought to encourage every one to bring their ponies, don't you? Then we can ride and jump from two o'clock till teatime, and that'll keep the guests occupied," suggested Augusta.

I remembered a certain sunlit day over a year ago, and I said: "I'm not so sure; it might be rather tiresome. Do you remember? No, of course you don't. You weren't there. I asked Charlie Dewhurst to tea once and she tried to jump Jingle over my jumps, with disastrous results. O'Neil appeared on the scene and waved his arms and gave bad advice, and in the end we nearly had a real row. I'm not sure it wouldn't be better to play tennis or hide and seek, or have a treasure hunt, not do anything with ponies—leave competitions for the club rallies when Eleanor is there to keep order."

"Your theory doesn't say much for our friends, does it?" remarked Augusta.

"Well, you suggested asking Terence and Mike, and quite honestly, I think if we do any riding they'll break up my jumps and upset Clown," I said, remembering a pillow fight in the moonlight and Terence struggling, filled with the terror of the helpless, in a deep and treacherous well.

"It needs careful thought," said Augusta, and we rode on in silence until we reached the road and realised that evening was upon us and that we had been foolish not to canter where the going had been good and that I had ridden Clown as though he was a staid old hunter, turning in the saddle to shout to Augusta, dangling and waving my legs—in fact in a thoroughly absent-minded and unorthodox manner.

Augusta said this was a good sign and that she thought that nine times out of ten if you rode a pony as though you expected him to misbehave, he *did* misbehave, and vice versa. The sun was setting in the glory of gold and crimson when we turned up the drive of Hampton House.

D

Chapter 12 by Augusta

DURING THE NEXT DAY we installed Clown in my orchard—or, to be more accurate, my parents' orchard. In many ways it was silly to turn him out to grass when the Chilswood Show was drawing so near, but lately he had been considerably fresher and inclined to buck and we had come to the conclusion that more freedom might improve his nerves and make him quieter. Mummy and Daddy were very decent and, in spite of Clown's lack of tact—he grabbed and ate an apple-laden bough as soon as he was turned loose— said that it was nice for Daybreak to have a companion and pleasant to see two ponies about the place. The Carrs were also pleased with this new arrangement; they had not really approved of Christina mucking out a stable and, in spite of Philip Lockheed's valuable advice and assistance, they were not very agreeably disposed towards Clown. But I think that, of everybody, I was, perhaps, the most pleased.

I thought that I was the luckiest person in the world when I wakened on the following morning and saw, through my white sash-window, the two ponies grazing side by side with an air of perfect contentment. Beneath the hundred-year-old Blenheims, they looked handsome but mysterious, with the mist that came with dawn still hovering around them, and the trees seeming strange and giant-like.

For months I had regretted Daybreak's loneliness, but, because hay is so expensive, I could never consider adopting a pensioner or taking my few small savings out to buy a sucker as a companion for him, and in the summer grazing round our way is plentiful, so no one ever wanted to turn their youngster out in our inferior grass. Now, hearing the squelch of eight feet in the dew and the pleasant sound of munching, I too felt contented.

While dressing, I remembered that we had planned to ride over to Nigel's house for tea and I began to wonder what his rooms were like. I imagined leather arm-chairs, oak bookcases and carved chests and pictures after Blake—a queer, unsuitable mixture. Looking round houses is a mania of mine. I think I'll be the agents' bug-bear when I'm grown up; one of those people who are for ever demanding keys and being taken round houses, which they have no intention of buying.

We reached Nigel's place at four after a delightful and uneventful ride, and before venturing indoors, we turned the ponies, Clown and Serenade, out in his field with Skiddaw. They rolled, squealed rudely at each other and nibbled the beech hedge, but took no notice of the goat, who was tethered by the garden gate. We watched them for a while, and then Nigel said: "Well, I think a little food might be a good idea, don't you?" and we went in to tea, and my curiosity was temporarily satisfied.

I do not think that I have ever been in a house which possessed such a civilised air as Nigel's house. He did not show us round as Piers and Tilly had done; we only saw the drawing-room, dining-room and hall, but each gave the same impression of elegance and culture. Nigel is an only child, and sitting on a Chippendale chair, with a Hepplewhite dresser opposite me and a glass-fronted bookcase behind, I thought I began to realise why he always seems old, almost learned for his age. You could not carpenter in this house for fear of knocking over some fragile piece of furniture; you could not paint for fear of spilling something on the Persian rugs or Turkey carpet; you could not play hide-and-seek for fear of dislodging some valuable china object. But you could sit and read until the cows came home. The mahogany bookcase in the dining-room, the white bookcases on either side of the fireplace in the drawing-room, all the shelves in the hall were full of books; even the passage had a cupboard of them.

His parents' conversation at tea seemed grown up, even for grown-ups. After asking us a few polite questions, they discussed architecture, life after death and the Bible. They mentioned the views of philosophers of whom I had never before heard, and Nigel occasionally joined in the conversation for a few moments, and managed to sound just as grown up as the others. It seemed very strange to me to hear parents talking to each other of such things. Normally, in my experience, parents keep to everyday happenings— the weather, the garden, the increase in income tax, their children's bad behaviour, the latest murder case and such topics.

By the time tea was over I was deep in a maze of thought, and Christina said "We are going out to look at the ponies now" three times before I heard her, jumped from my chair, and then, realising my ill-mannered silence, plunged into irrelevant talk.

The ponies were earnestly grazing the other side of the field to Skiddaw, which was disappointing, because we had hoped, stupidly enough, to find them firm friends. Nigel said that, since goats were rarely, if ever, engaged in circus work, one could not expect Clown to wish to indulge in their company. Christina said that Nigel was just trying to be irritating and knew perfectly well that Clown had no reason whatsoever to be interested in circuses. They had a short argument while I caught the ponies, and then we spent a lively hour persuading Serenade and Clown to touch Skiddaw. Eventually we succeeded in this task, and after Christina had jumped her mount over Nigel's only jump and we had both thanked our hostess and hosts, we turned for home.

The ride back seemed longer than before, partly, I suppose, because we did not make a break at Hampton House, but rode right on to Bumpers, where my faithful Lucifer was waiting in the yard for my return. The ponies behaved well and we agreed that we had not been unreasonably rash in entering Clown for the Under 14.2 Showing Class at Chilswood. Christina came up to the stable door with me, so that Clown should have no reason to jib. He seemed tired and hungry now and, remembering that our orchard grass is of rather poor quality, I fetched him a big feed of oats, bran and chaff, but for some reason unknown to me forgot that he might be thirsty. Because of my stupidity, he did not drink until he had eaten and I had turned him out with Daybreak in the orchard, where there is a whole bath full of water at the ponies' disposal. I think I must have been in a dream that hot July evening, because I also failed to notice the yellowing pile of lawn mowings by the gate; and either of these two things—the long drink after the feed or the mowings—might have caused what happened later.

Supper was over, the plates, cutlery and glasses back clean in their places. Mummy was knitting and reading, Daddy writing letters and I looking through the latest copy of *Riding*, revelling in the fresh smell of new shiny paper and admiring an article on Arab stallions. The gay summer curtains were undrawn and night was blue at the window, and there seemed no noise or movement from without the house; while within only the sharp metallic click of tireless needles and the scarcely audible sound of pen on paper broke the companionable silence.

Then suddenly Lucifer, the light sleeper, wakened and, running to the door, barked hysterically.

"What*ever's* the matter? Do you suppose there's any one outside?" asked Mummy, raising her eyes from the latest Simenon book, but continuing her knitting.

"I had better go and see," said Daddy. "I don't know why it is, but whenever I begin to write letters something must interrupt me—very curious." He rose with a grunt and left the room, Lucifer close on his heels. A moment later he called me, saying that there was trouble in the orchard; he thought a horse was rolling rather wildly, and Lucifer was still barking under the trees.

Of course, I could not find a torch, and I ran out into the darkness without a light and scratched my face on a low apple branch. A pony certainly *was* rolling and the pony was Clown, and I thought—colic. For although I had never seen a horse in the throes of colic, I had read of the symptoms many times, and one of them is violent rolling. Saying "Whoa, steady there," I ran to Clown's head and he scrambled to his feet and stood trembling. I always have a few oats in my pockets, much to Mummy's annoyance because I spill them on the floor when I take a handkerchief out, and I offered him a handful, but with no success; he would not consider eating them.

A golden blob of light approached from behind, causing Clown to snort and trot away into the darkness; it was Mummy and Daddy with a torch.

"Anything the matter?" they asked.

"I think he might have got colic. He's rolling. There, look! He's down again," I cried, seeing Clown's white patches meet the dark ground. Daddy grabbed Lucifer, who was beginning to bark again.

"Why don't you catch the pony? I've brought a belt and a carrot," said Mummy.

"I should give it some castor oil or does it need the vet, Augusta?" asked Daddy.

"You don't know the first thing, Peter," said Mummy, laughing. "One doesn't give ponies castor oil, does one?"

"Well, paraffin or whatever you *do* give them then."

"I think what he needs is a colic drink," I said, "but I haven't got any. Usually you give them one, and then, if they are not better in an hour, you give them another, or call the vet in, I think. I'll try to catch

86

him, anyway. Can you stand still, please, because your torch frightens him. I'll see if he'll have the carrot?"

Slowly, making the foolish sort of remarks one makes to calm ill or nervous ponies, I walked through the dew-wet grass to the rolling skewbald. Why do things like this have to happen at night? I wondered. When I was quite close, Clown leaped to his feet, and I realised that he had not quite overcome his fear of the human race. But seeing that it was me, he stood still while I put the belt round his hot, damp neck and tried in vain to persuade him to eat the carrot.

"Have you got him?" called Mummy, and I answered, "Yes, thank you," and led Clown slowly and mournfully to the stable, which, luckily, has an electric light. Daybreak followed as far as the gate and then, finding himself shut alone in the orchard, started neighing frantically and galloping up and down the fence.

Before I could spread the straw in the loose-box, Clown started to roll and, remembering that one of my books had hinted that if a horse was allowed to roll violently when suffering from colic he might twist a gut, I became alarmed and, pulling him to his feet, persuaded Mummy to spread the straw.

Daddy said: "Well, as there doesn't seem much that I can do, I think I will finish my letters," and went indoors.

"Why don't you ring up Christina and ask her if she has a colic drink? She could always bring O'Neil to look at him," said Mummy.

"That's an idea. Whoa, Clown; you mustn't roll. Oh dear, he does seem ill. Perhaps we ought to have the vet," I said, watching him kick at his tummy and glance nervously in the direction of his flank. "I wonder if I ought to lead him up and down."

"Well, look," said Mummy, "we'll put a rug over him and you can lead him about while I ring up Christina; after all, the pony's her responsibility as well as yours."

She fetched Daybreak's night rug and then disappeared into the house, leaving me alone with Clown and my own apprehensions. The pony would barely walk now; each moment he wanted to lie down and it was all I could do to keep him on his feet. We went outside into the yard, where the light threw a shaft of gold across the gravel and a light breeze fanned our faces. My gosh, I thought, I fed him before watering him—that must have caused it. Supposing he dies, dies just because I was absent-minded. Oh, why

Supposing he dies

was I so silly? Oh, the poor fellow; he's in such pain. I wish Mummy would hurry up. Perhaps we really ought to have the vet. I wish I had a colic drink. Perhaps the Carrs will bring one. Supposing he does twist a gut? He'll die in awful agony and it'll be all my beastly fault for daydreaming. I wish Mummy would hurry up.

I imagined the gut like a piece of chitterling, only

blue where it was twisted. I felt the dew falling again; it seemed to drip off the trees and touch my hair and stay there, damp and sticky. Behind the quiet stables, like a queen, the moon rose, and over the sleeping meadows, across our little crooked orchard, came the chime of the church bell, striking ten o'clock.

Chapter 13 by Christina

WHEN MRS. THORNEDYKE rang up, my parents and I were watching a film which Daddy had made in the Easter holidays. It was of a horse show and most of the riding club members were in some of the shots, and suddenly I gave a shriek and said could Augusta and I show it at our party? Daddy said yes, and as he spoke the telephone bell rang. Walters answered as usual and then called me.

Mrs. Thornedyke explained the situation in a few words and presently my parents, O'Neil and myself were well on the road to Bumpers, with two colic drinks in the car. It was an incredibly lovely evening and, as we drove through the quiet country, between the dim, sleepy banks, the moon rose and gilded the dew on the hedges silver; and somewhere high above our heads a nightingale poured forth his song, and the rabbits scuttled from the road back to the sheltered fields and their burrows, and even the uglier cottages became pleasantly beautiful. I felt that this drive was strangely like a description I had read in a book, in which a nightingale had sung from branches tipped silver by the moon.

Daddy did not seem to realise the need for urgency and, carried away by the loveliness of the night, he suggested that we should stop awhile and listen to the song. But O'Neil and I were firm and soon we saw the tiles of Bumpers, and then, turning the corner, the stable light and figures in the yard. O'Neil was out of the car first and at Clown's side in a moment. After taking a look at the pony's eye, noting his heavy breathing and frequent glances towards his flank and stomach, O'Neil said:

"Put 'im in the box and we'll give him a drench."

Ten minutes of struggling followed, for Clown had no intention of swallowing the colic drink—a mixture of turpentine, linseed oil and, I believe, cloric ether, which O'Neil had got several months before from some vet or other. I stood on a bucket trying to keep Clown's head up, while Augusta tried to keep his quarters against the wall and O'Neil attempted to drench him from the manger. We managed to make him swallow twice, but a large quantity of liquid seemed to ooze out between his teeth and whenever I let him lower his head, he released an absolute flood of it. And then, suddenly, he decided that he had had enough and stood straight up on end. Mummy, who was in the doorway, shrieked: "Oh, darling, do be careful! Take care! He'll hit you with his fore feet." And Daddy said: 'I think we had better call in the vet." But O'Neil was calm. "Keep his head down, Miss," he advised, continuing operations—though unsuccessfully, for a moment later Clown reared again.

"He can't be feeling very low if he can stand up like that," Daddy remarked.

"It's spasmodic," explained Augusta; "one minute he seems better and begins to nibble the hedge or look in my pockets, and then the next he is trying to roll and kick his tummy."

"Ah, colic—that's what that is—dare say an enema will do him good," mused O'Neil.

"Mrs. Thornedyke, may we use your telephone and ring up a vet? Perhaps he can cure the brute," said Daddy.

"Not a brute," I contradicted.

"Of course, certainly, do come in." Augusta's mother started as though she had been in a maze of day-dreaming. "I'm afraid I've been dillying and dallying and not knowing whether to get a vet or not. Augusta said you were sure to have a colic drink and she thought it might just do the trick and, of course, I know so awfully little about ponies."

"Well, I've only had to deal with pedigree animals really, and with them it's the dillying and dallying which so often ends in a tragedy," said Daddy, following Mrs. Thornedyke down the path.

"Christina! You are to come away from that pony at *once*. I will not have you wounded on the head by his feet," said Mummy.

"Now, then, don't let him dribble it all out this time," ordered O'Neil, pushing the neck of the bottle between Clown's lips. "Ready, careful. Hold him!" Augusta and I struggled to hold the pony in place, but we struggled in vain; a moment later he started rearing again and then, pulling the rope out of my hands, dashed to the other end of the box.

"Christina, *will* you come out of there, at *once*. You'll get killed with that pony. I know you will. His ears are going back now. Do come out," cried Mummy.

"Go on. There's no point in staying," said Augusta.

"Righto, I'm coming, but honestly, Mummy, he's only frightened; he's not trying to bash my head in or anything," I said.

"Let's wait for the vet," suggested Augusta.

"I'll lead him up and down—best to keep them on the move," said O'Neil, bringing Clown out into the yard.

"He's sweating a bit," Augusta pointed out.

"What do you think can have caused the colic?" I asked.

"I don't know; it's difficult to say," answered Augusta, and then, after a pause, "except that I did a very silly thing. When you left this afternoon, I mean this evening, I gave him a big feed—a bucket full and mostly whole oats—and forgot to water him before, in fact he had no water in his box so that he could not even drink half-way. Then, like a fool, when he had finished eating I turned him out in the orchard, where he could drink gallons and gallons. That sort of thing causes colic, doesn't it?"

"I think it comes under the heading of Injudicious Feeding and Watering. I don't think one ought to give more than two pounds of oats in one feed to a pony anyway, ought one?" I asked, wishing that Daddy would soon return.

"I can't think why I was so stupid. I know perfectly well that what I did was wrong. I was just absent-minded, thinking of something else. Shall I lead him now, O'Neil?" said Augusta.

Daddy appeared from the house with Mrs. Thornedyke. "It's all settled," he told us in business-like tones. "The man said he couldn't come at first, because he was just off on an urgent case—got to attend to a cow or something. But I said that ours happened to be an urgent case too. The pony, though of no great value, was in pain, and my wife was afraid it would injure my daughter at any moment. He saw sense then and said that he would be along shortly, and I pointed out that it would be worth his while to oblige, because we have several valuable animals which are sure to need his attention from time to time. Now, you three come in and have some tea. Mrs. Thornedyke has very kindly made a pot, and O'Neil will see to the pony."

The vet must have seen the cow first, because he did not come along very shortly. His large bright head-lights did not turn up Bumpers drive until nearly eleven o'clock, when Clown was in pain again. Contrary to my expectations, he was an old man with a slight stoop and a brown wrinkled face and a sagging moustache. By the time we had hurried to the stables he had already looked at Clown and spoken a few words with O'Neil.

"Good evening," he greeted us with the shadow of a smile. "A case of spasmodic colic, I think. Has any one any theory as to what the cause may have been? He's

93

in too good condition to have been suffering from worms; most likely some indigestible form of food has brought the attack on—fomenting lawn mowings, frozen grass; that sort of thing can cause colic, you know." He glanced at Clown's flank and added: "He's not so bad though."

"Oh!" said Mrs. Thornedyke. "He's been able to eat mown grass. My husband chucked some out last week when he had finished the lawn."

O'Neil gave a snort of disapproval.

"And I did a silly thing," said Augusta sheepishly. "I gave him a big feed after work and no water; and then, when he had eaten, let him drink as much as he liked."

"I see, yes. Thank you. Well, either might have brought on this attack. Now I'll fetch something out of the car." He returned a few moments later with a hypodermic and injected Clown.

"This eserine," he said, "acts as a purgative. You say you got a little colic drink down him—the usual, I suppose—mostly linseed oil and turpentine?"

"That's right, sir," replied O'Neil.

"Good. Well, now I should let him lie down, if he wants to, and rest; but don't allow violent rolling. I'll wait for a while; if that stuff does its job, he should show some improvement within forty minutes."

We all stood in the loose-box and Daddy talked to the vet, mostly about the price of cars, and our two mothers talked to each other, and O'Neil to Clown, and Augusta and I were silent. I must say all the grown-ups, except for the vet, looked odd and out of place in the surroundings. Mrs. Thornedyke's faded cotton frock and sandals were not suitable garb for the stable, and Mummy's high heels and silk and Daddy's dark town suit seemed ridiculous in the setting of dim whitewashed walls, rafters and cobwebs and deep, clean straw. Even O'Neil was not dressed for the part. He had just returned from seeing his relatives, when we fetched him from his cottage, and he was wearing a very shiny blue, pin-stripe suit.

Presently Clown lay down and, watching his laboured breathing and uneasy eye, I was glad that Ted Dunne was not here to witness the pony's suffering. O'Neil pulled his ears gently and murmured calming words. The vet, tired of cars and money, said: "He's not a bad sort of animal, you know—nice limbs he's got and not such a bad front either."

"Not up to show standard, though, lacks quality—wouldn't you say so?" asked Daddy.

"Well, he's not quite a blood pony, but a good type all the same—right sort for a child."

Augusta's face lit up with pleasure.

"Indeed!" exclaimed Mummy. "You should have seen him a little while before you came; he was behaving like a mad thing. I was afraid he would knock Christina's head in."

"Most animals play up when they are being drenched," said Daddy in a knowing manner, "but, admittedly, Clown was a handful when these two girls got him, but Christina has been well taught and Augusta's got sense, and, between them, I think they'll make a very good job."

"Splendid," said the vet, while Augusta turned slightly red and I felt a fool and fiddled with my belt.

After that remark conversation petered out and all eyes turned to Clown. The injection of eserine had achieved the desired results and he obviously began to feel better.

Augusta's and my thoughts turned again to the Chilswood Show. I had entered Symphony for the Best Pony Class, so Augusta was going to ride Clown; we were not expecting him to win anything, but hoped that he would behave well. I could imagine him now, rearing in the collecting ring, backing into the judges, jumping over the ropes; and I wondered, as I was to wonder many times before Bank Holiday, whether we had been right in entering him.

Strange though it may seem, the vet's mind seemed to have turned in the same direction, for he told us that he was acting as honorary vet at the Chilswood Show and asked whether we would be competing. Daddy answered before I had collected my wits, and by the time he had explained everything that he could explain about my ponies and the show, Clown was up and eating hay.

"Seems as though he's all right, sir," said O'Neil.

"Yes, I think I can leave you now," the vet answered. "The pony should go on well, but someone had better be around in case he takes a turn for the worse. I think we can safely say that the colic was caused either by a large quantity of water, drunk after a substantial feed of whole oats, or by fomenting lawn mowings. If anything should go wrong, give me a ring and I'll be out at once."

We thanked him rather profusely, and in return he gave us a wan smile and then left the stable, Daddy following.

"I'll sit up with Clown," said Augusta.

"I'm sure O'Neil would rather *he* did it," said Mummy.

"But we agreed to look after the pony and I think we ought to keep the bargain. We've had lots of help for one night, thank you very much," I answered.

"O'Neil is the only one of us who has not had a cup of tea and a slice of cake. Will you come in now and have one?" suggested Mrs. Thornedyke.

"Thank you, Madam—I will."

He left the stable and the two of them went away down the path.

"I don't see why he should sit up all night. He's not employed to look after Clown. Anyway, Augusta and I will enjoy watching the darkness turn to dawn and he won't; he'll wish he was back in his little cottage and he'll say to himself, 'I knew this would happen. They were so sure they were going to look after the blooming pony, but as soon as anything goes wrong, round they come as weak as water,' " I told Mummy.

"Well, I suppose if Mrs. Thornedyke wants Augusta to sit up all night, she can; but I'm not having you doing it and that's that; and I'm quite sure your father will agree with me," she answered firmly.

"I think that's much the best idea—all of you and O'Neill go home and I stay with Clown. It's so much easier for me—I mean, seeing that I live at Bumpers anyway," said Augusta.

Then Daddy returned and Mummy said: "It's not right for Christina to stay up here all night in the stable, is it?" and he replied: "Good gracious no. What do we employ a groom for?"

"To look after Symphony, Serenade and Solo, *not* Clown. Oh, *need* I go home, please? I don't see why I shouldn't stay and I'm sure O'Neil wants to get back. His wife is probably getting most awfully anxious—imagines we've had a crash or something," I said.

Then Mrs. Thornedyke returned and settled the matter. "Augusta and I will watch Clown," she said. "Don't any of you bother. I know Mr. O'Neil wants to get back; he's just told me so. His wife's one of the nervy sort. I haven't got anything special on to-morrow, so Augusta and I can always have a snooze in the afternoon if we are absolutely exhausted, which I don't suppose we will be."

Daddy needed little more persuasion, and ten minutes later we were driving back down the now dark lanes to Hampton House. A wonderful stillness lay over the land; it seemed to me that every one for miles around must be asleep. There were no lighted windows, no tired hurrying bicyclists, no other cars; I believe even the clouds were stationary and, although I leaned out, I could not hear a single rustle.

When we reached home, Shannan was nearly crazy with delight. He did not bark, although he can make such a terrific noise; he put his great paws on to my shoulders and gave little mouse-like cries, and then,

97

E

when I had patted him and explained that he need not have worried, he dashed up and down stairs and in and out of the rooms like a mad thing; and his pleasure at my return consoled me a little for I was still sorry that I had not stayed with Augusta.

Next morning Clown had completely recovered.

Chapter 14 by Augusta

I SHALL NOT EASILY FORGET the Chilswood Show; the morning that dawned so unbelievably fair; the first cock's shrill clarion that rent the air and started the birds singing; the feel of the early dew soaking through my sandshoes, as I caught the ponies in our misty orchard; the arrival of Christina, looking so comic and unsafe on Martha's bicycle, which I had borrowed; our struggles with Clown, who did not want to be washed or plaited; our hasty breakfast of fried eggs and potatoes—all these things seemed stored in my memory and I have only to think "Bank Holiday" for them to come crowding back into my mind, as though it was but yesterday. And yet I do not want to remember the show or our preparations for it, the day that ended not tragically, but disappointingly. It was the very fact that it started so successfully that made the finish seem worse than it was; for, until eleven o'clock, everything pointed to our luck being in. As I left the stable yard a ladybird, superbly neat and beautiful, alighted on my arm, where she remained for nearly an hour. A few moments later we saw a black cat, and when we reached the showground I found that I had been wearing my socks inside out.

"Never," said I, "have two people met with so many good omens in so short a time."

Christina found her three ponies, which O'Neil had insisted upon preparing for the show unaided, very quickly. They had travelled to Chilswood in a new and superior horse-box and I must say they did look smart, much smarter than Clown or Daybreak. Serenade's socks seemed as white as the whitest snow, and his coat shone like a dark and polished conker. Solo, hogged and docked, the colour of roasted coffee beans, looked like the perfect cob, and Symphony's coat seemed pure glistening gold. Their hoofs were oiled, their legs were being unbandaged and the tops of their tails were still encased in smart tail-guards. I could hardly believe that they were the same ponies as I had been riding a few days ago; they looked far too smart.

The Pony Showing Class was the first. Mummy, who had driven over in her battered Baby Austin, kindly tied Daybreak to a post while I rode Clown round outside the ring. He was nervous and inclined to get behind the bit. I was frightened that he might rear, so I kept him on the move and we proceeded at rather a meandering trot.

Presently Christina and Symphony joined us and then, a few moments later, we were called into the collecting ring. Several of our club members were here. There was Phyllis riding Swallow, Tilly on Seaspray, Pat and Heather with their two ponies, Amber and Dawn, Mike with Nightmare, Terrence with Sootie, and Tony Allbright on his well-known show pony, Melonie. Then there were about ten people whom I did not know at all; one of whom was riding an attractive pinky-grey pony, which looked as though it was half Arab. I pointed him out to Christina as a rival for Symphony, but she said that Symphony had beaten him in a big show in the Easter holidays. Tony Allbright admired Clown's markings, but the Folley twins said he was a bit straight in front. Phyllis nearly drove herself into hysteria, because a horse-fly settled on Swallow's tummy, but was eventually rescued by Nigel, complete with Gruffy, his pug, and Punch. Of course, I was tortured by the needle—so much in fact that I could hardly speak. Christina seemed calm and walked Symphony up and down some distance away from the other ponies, and because she is experienced in the art of showing ponies, I soon followed her example. Clown felt remarkably quiet; I think he was thinking deeply; anyway, he followed his chestnut friend with docile obedience, until at long last we were called into the ring—then the fun began. When showing, Christina always likes to lead the way, or, at any rate, not be farther back than third. As it happened on this occasion, Tony Allbright, who has competed at Richmond, went first, and it was only by dashing across the collecting ring that she managed to fall in second. We had planned that Clown should follow Symphony in this class, but I was slow in the uptake, and by the time I had reached the ring there were already two strangers following her, so I tried to fall in fourth. And now Clown began to take charge; he looked at the jumps, at the small crowd by the ring ropes, at the two farmer judges, and then swung round on his hocks and dashed to Amber, as though seeking her protection.

"Don't, August," cried Pat. "He's dirtying my jodhs. Take the beastly skewbald animal away."

"Sorry," I said, trying in vain to force Clown back to the ring entrance.

"Can't you control him?" asked Pat a moment later.

"I don't seem to be able to now," I answered, using my legs vigorously.

"I suppose you had better follow me then." Pat and Heather rode into the ring and I once again got as far as the entrance, where Clown reared, swung round and placed himself beside Phyllis, who shrieked:

"Oh dear, *please* don't upset Swallow. I implore you, Augusta, please go away."

"You go in," I said hopefully, "and I'll follow."

"Oh, but I wanted to go last," wailed Phyllis, "so that Swallow won't kick any one."

"Well, I'll keep well away from you and then he won't be able to kick Clown," I told her.

"Oh dear, all right then." She obligingly rode into the ring and, to my intense relief, I managed to follow and for a while all went well.

It was early yet for spectators and only a few people were at the ring ropes, and it was not long before I noticed that Ted Dunne was one of them. He nodded as I passed, but made no remark, and, calling out "Good morning," I felt even more determined to show Clown successfully. Winning did not matter, I decided; all I wanted was to be called into the front line and, if possible, told that my pony had nice manners, but needed a little more schooling.

Presently we were told to trot and then to canter, and, to my surprise and relief, Clown led off on the right leg. But once cantering he became hard to control; I felt him stiffen all over, until his back seemed almost as though it was arched and his neck like a plank, and instead of sitting *in* the saddle I seemed to be on *top* of it.

Phyllis was cantering very slowly and collectedly; and in a few minutes I had passed her and the Folleys, and was bearing down on Melonie and Symphony, who were proceeding with dignity and grace, as befitted two such well-known show ponies. And then, suddenly, the microphone was switched on and through an amplifier, cunningly fixed in the boughs of a noble oak, came the most alarming burring sound. And the next moment my hat had gone; Clown's mouth had become as insensitive as a piece of wood and we were going round the ring at a gallop. I tried taking sharp, short pulls at the reins; I tried taking long pulls; I tried using my legs and keeping my hands still—but all in vain. Each minute, our gallop became faster, until we had passed Melonie and Symphony a second time and were catching up with Swallow again. I saw the judges' faces become anxious. I noticed Christina's alarmed expression; I dared not glance towards the ring ropes for fear that I might see Ted Dunne.

"Steady, Augusta, *please*. You'll upset Swallow. *Do*

We were going round the ring at a gallop

stop," implored Phyllis, clutching hold of her saddle's pommel with one hand.

"Hard luck," said Mike.

"Oooo, er! Look at that pony," exclaimed a spectator.

"Coo, can't 'e move!" commented another.

"Walk every one," ordered the taller and thinner of the two judges. "Come in, you on the skewbald."

What a hopeless request, I thought, and with the sound of Clown's thudding hoofs in my ears, I pulled more frantically at his mouth. Never before had I felt so helpless. I seemed to have galloped for an age. I lost all sense of time. I dared not look at any one. The other competitors broke into a walk.

"Jump off," advised Terrence.

"Oh, *do* stop," wailed Phyllis.

"Can't you pull him up?" called Heather.

"Turn him round," said Christina, as I passed her for the third time.

"Come in, my dear—into the middle," called the smaller judge kindly.

Then Clown swerved and I saw the entrance of the ring before me and the green acres of Chilswood Park. I tried to turn him back towards the judges, but in two strides he was out of the ring, and the next moment we were galloping across the show-ground with the gentle westerly wind in our faces; and then I saw Mummy and for some reason Clown stopped.

"What *are* you trying to do?" asked Mummy.

"Ride nicely round the ring," I answered and, dismounting, explained what had happened.

Mummy was decent, of course. She is not the sort of parent who wants her child to win constantly; she likes gymkhanas to be more a pleasure than a toil and she is not ashamed if I make a fool of myself. She did not say "What will people think?" or "You should have stopped him," or "Darling, you might have been killed," or "The brute must be sold," as some parents might have done. Instead, with the utmost calm, she said: "He looks terribly hot. I expect he'll be better next time. Was it the microphone, do you think?"

"I don't know," I said. "Oh, good, here's someone bringing my crash cap."

A steward approached across the showground with my hat under his arm, and as he reached me the first spots of rain started to fall.

Chapter 15 by Christina

I MUST SAY I was glad when Augusta did not bring
Clown back into the ring. I had felt awful watching
her gallop round completely out of control; seeing her
hat fly off and her hair stand on end, and hearing Tony
Allbright's "That kid shouldn't be allowed in the ring,"
and Phyllis moaning miserably because she was afraid
that Clown would frighten Swallow. I felt mean, too,
because I had persuaded her that he had more chance
of winning the class than Daybreak. I had soon realised
that we had been very silly to enter our pupil at all—
let alone in a rubber snaffle—and I wished, with all
my heart, that Ted Dunne was not at the ring ropes.

I was so intent watching Augusta's wild retreat across
the showground to Mrs. Thornedyke, that I did not
notice my fellow competitors, and when I turned my
attention back to the ring and judges the steward
beckoned to me, and I was surprised to see that
Melonie and the pinky-grey pony, which was named
Dream Boy, had already been called into the middle.

I joined them and we stood in a row trying to make
our ponies look as handsome as possible. Symphony
was restless; she gazed in the direction that Clown had
gone, champed her bit and fidgeted. Presently, a girl
on a pretty chestnut with a flaxen mane and tail, a
small boy on a well-built but rather heavy grey gelding,
Mike on Nightmare and Phyllis on Swallow joined us
in that order. And, after the other competitors had
been asked to make a back row, we privileged seven
were told, each in turn, to canter a figure of eight. I
think Melonie, Dream Boy, the little chestnut and

106

Symphony all performed well; but Swallow brought Phyllis back to the front row when they reached the middle of their figure of eight; Nightmare careered round with his weight on his forehand, and the stocky grey refused to canter on the near leg.

The judges asked us to ride in a small circle in single file and then, after a few moments' conversation, the rosettes were awarded—Melonie the red, Dream Boy the blue and Symphony the yellow.

Outside the ring once more, I found Augusta, who

Christina showing Symphony

was full of apologies and, although I did not feel inclined to talk about Clown, I stayed and chatted because I was trying to put off the moment when I must hear Daddy's and O'Neil's disappointed remarks for I knew that they would think that I should have won the class. But evil moments can rarely be postponed for ever and my parents and groom soon found me.

"Never seen such judging!" said O'Neil. "What, that odd-coloured pony put above Symphony! It's ridiculous. The boy couldn't ride properly either."

"It was that skewbald brute that upset Symphony. You know, she was changing feet all the way round," said Daddy.

"Never mind, darling; it's only a little show. They tell me the taller judge is quite ignorant, only a farmer who does a bit of dealing in horses now and then," said Mummy, and then, turning to Augusta, "And you did have a gallop, *didn't* you? What upset Clown?"

"It might have been the microphone, I suppose. My only consolation is that at least I have helped to give the spectators their money's worth. Most of them seemed to think it the funniest John Gilpin act that they had seen for a long time," Augusta replied.

"Well, we are told that 'it's an ill wind that blows nobody any good,' aren't we? But I must say I didn't envy you," said Mummy.

"The brute's no good, Christina," said Daddy.

"It's only his first time," I told him.

"Darling, look, it's beginning to rain quite hard. Do come into the dry or fetch a mac or something," said Mummy.

"Hard luck, August," called Mike and Terrence, trotting by.

"I thought you were riding from Aix to Ghent," said Nigel.

"I'm going to buttonhole the judges and find out why they only gave Symphony third," said Daddy.

"Oh no, please don't. One must expect judges to differ; otherwise showing would be no fun at all. I've no desire to win every time. I can think of nothing worse. Anyway, Symphony *wasn't* going really well and Melonie *was*." I spoke emphatically, for on no account did I want Daddy to bother the judges.

"I'm just going to ride Clown round for a few moments, and then I'm going to get Daybreak ready for the jumping," said Augusta, mounting.

"Plucky child," said Mummy. "Daddy, Christina, I insist that you should both come and put on mackintoshes at once and eat your lunch in the car out of the rain."

We did as we were bade, and after I had eaten I helped Augusta saddle and bridle Daybreak. And then O'Neil brought me the sad news that Serenade was lame. I knew at that moment that, for Augusta and I, this day would be a flop. It began to rain harder and Daybreak turned his back to the wind. The Folleys galloped by on Amber and Dawn.

"Don't you think I might jump Symphony instead?" I asked.

"Oh no, I shouldn't do that. She's too good for jumping, and she didn't do well at that cock-eyed club show. You'll only spoil her; and I'm sure your father will say the same."

"All right, I won't," I said, for I knew it was no good arguing with my parents *and* O'Neil, and, anyway, it was ten to one that, in this rain, Symphony would refuse three times and then they would all be furious with me.

I looked at Serenade, but could find no heat in his lame leg. I will not describe my feelings, for I am sure you can well imagine them. In fact, I'm not going to dwell on August Bank Holiday afternoon for long, because this book is about Clown and he did not compete in any of the events.

I do not think Augusta and I are the sort of children who only enjoy gymkhanas if they win prizes. It was the cold and pelting rain and the minor tragedies which succeeded one another with steady persistence which depressed us and made the day seem unenjoyable.

The Children's Jumping Class was won by Tilly Lockewood on Seaspray, which pleased us all. Daybreak was fifth with four faults. He slipped on the take off in front of the gate, which he knocked down with his fore legs. At the last minute Phyllis had an attack of nerves and asked me to ride Swallow round the course instead of herself. I hesitated and then accepted, telling her that my luck was out. Although I used my legs vigorously, Swallow refused the triple bars three times and we were disqualified. I left the ring feeling that I had ridden badly and let Phyllis down.

Daddy said that I should not accept rides on dubious mounts and that I had made a fool of myself.

The Children's Jumping was followed by Novice Jumping and then three races—Bending, Potato and V.C. Race—in which I was riding Solo.

By this time it was pouring with rain; I was nearly soaked to the skin and my parents were both convinced that I should scratch and go home. Solo was nearly as miserable as a pony can be. His ears are very sensitive and he cannot bear the rain on them; each drop seems to sting him. On this afternoon he carried his head between his knees and at every opportunity turned round so that his back was to the wind.

Waiting in the collecting ring, every one, except Phyllis, tried to appear cheerful. We felt each other's clothes and tried to decide which of us was the wettest. We squeezed the water from the sleeves of our coats and shrieked when the rain trickled down our necks.

Augusta and I were put together in the first heat of the Bending Race, which was disappointing because we can and do practise against each other at home. On the word *go* Solo forgot the rain and shot forward in his usual style. We were first to reach the end, but as we turned his feet slipped, and the next moment both Solo and I were on the ground. We were not hurt, but we had lost the race and alarmed Mummy. Heather Folley won the heat, for although Daybreak finished first he had knocked down a post and was therefore disqualified.

The whole race was eventually won by the girl and the chestnut pony, which had competed in the Showing Class, and Piers and Seaspray were second, and Mike and Nightmare third.

The Potato Race was next, and Mummy and I had

rather an undignified argument in the collecting ring about whether I should enter or not. Mummy said that Solo would fall down again and I should hit my head and be concussed. I said that Solo had learned his lesson now and would take great care to stay on his feet. Luckily Daddy, Augusta and O'Neil supported me, and eventually Mummy gave way. Solo *was* careful, but I wasn't; throwing recklessly, I missed the bucket with my potato and was beaten by Terrence, who, for some unknown reason, seemed to think that to defeat Solo and myself was a special triumph. Afterwards he went round telling every one that he had *even beaten Christina.* Daybreak kicked Augusta's bucket over and her heat was won by Pat Folley, who finally won the whole competition, beating Mike, who was second, by a short head.

I need hardly say that, from Augusta's and my point of view, the V.C. Race was not a success. We had to carry sacks filled with straw from one end of the ring to the other, jumping a flight of hurdles on the way. Not only was Solo terrified by the sack, but he refused the hurdles, and we finished last. Augusta stupidly forgot to tighten her girths, so that when she mounted with her sack her saddle slipped and she sat down in the mud. This event was won by a local farmer's son called Tom Blake; Piers was second and Pat Folley third.

It was still raining when we left the showground, raining as though it had not rained for months, as though the clouds had been busy for ages filling themselves with water for the special purpose of soaking every one in England on Bank Holiday.

I am sorry to say that we were gloomy, gloomier than we should have been, and then Augusta made matters worse by remembering, half-way home, that she had left her only jack-knife and a new dandy brush under a tree in Chilswood Park. She gave a shriek of exasperation; she was particularly sorry about the knife, which had been given to her by a godmother

111

last Christmas, because she thought it would be years before she could buy another one like it.

"Never in the history of Man have so many minor tragedies beset two children in one day," said Augusta —"that is, if they can *beset*."

Then suddenly we began to laugh. "We are doomed," I said. "Come on, let's sing and forget them."

The ponies seemed infected by our change of mood; they jogged now at intervals and carried their heads high, in spite of the cruel rain. We sang old-fashioned but cheerful songs like "Tipperary" and "Keep right on to the end of the Road," and when, at eight o'clock, we reached Bumpers, we were cold, wet, but surprisingly gay.

Chapter 16 by Augusta

WE SPENT THE DAY after Bank Holiday discussing our future treatment of Clown and writing out invitations for our party, which we had decided to hold in a week's time.

We agreed that Clown must now be given more schooling and less hacking and, after rather a heated argument, that we would keep him in a rubber snaffle for a little longer.

"I'm quite sure that it was nerves that made him misbehave yesterday, and when he gets more confidence in us and obeys our aids without thinking, he'll be all right," said Christina.

We sent this invitation to my cousins, the Lockewoods, Nigel, the Folleys, Mike, Terrence and Phyllis:

Christina Carr and Augusta Thornedyke request the pleasure of your company at Hampton House on August 10th for tea and supper. 2.30—p.m. Please wear jodhs or slacks or ancient frocks, and bring a dog if you possess one. R.S.V.P.

"If people come in party clothes it will be awful. We won't be able to climb trees or run through brambles or anything," said Christina.

"Dogs are a help when conversation lags and, seeing that we are not riding, we can always make them jump," I said.

We forgot Charlie Dewhurst—Christina's pet aversion; but not for long. Within three days she had heard about our party and, meeting us riding Clown and Solo,

113

she said: "You are beasts; I believe you've purposely not invited me."

Charlie is so outspoken that sometimes I can't help admiring her. She never seems frightened of saying anything to anybody. Christina and I were so surprised that we just sat with our mouths open, looking, I should imagine, like village idiots. Getting no answer, she screwed up her freckled face and continued: "Is it because you don't like Terry? I know he annoyed your cat last time, Chris."

Terry is Charlie's Irish terrier, a naughty dog with no manners.

"Don't call me Chris," said Christina angrily. There was a pause now and Charlie looked hard at me. I don't like her, but I felt that, having invited all the other camp members, it would be a bit mean to leave her out.

"Sorry; we forgot you," I said. "I don't know how we managed to be so remiss. Of course we would like you to come; and bring Terry. We are going to shut Ferkin up anyway."

Christina was furious with me afterwards.

"I don't want to be mean, but she's such a beastly grabbing child. She's not a friend; she couldn't be anybody's friend; she's hard-boiled; she'll spoil everything with her horrid remarks. I do wish you hadn't invited her. You sounded pretty false, too," Christina complained.

"You wait till you see my cousins," I warned. "If any one's hard-boiled, Jill is; and *you* made me ask them to come."

"Oh gosh! It's going to be an awful party. For goodness' sake let's talk about something else. Wasn't it lucky that Ted Dunne didn't come and comment on Clown's behaviour at Chilswood? I was terrified that he would say he wanted him back."

"*Don't* let's talk about the show. How's Serenade by the way?"

"You are an escapist. The vet says he's throwing a splint. O'Neil's terribly upset, but Daddy keeps being grateful that it isn't Symphony."

"Poor Serenade. Why on earth should he, of all ponies, get a splint? You never work him hard."

"Nobody knows. It's not as though he's ever strained his tendons or been kicked, or suddenly brought up from grass and put into strenuous work—most strange. We are just waiting now until the splint arrives; then we'll see what can be done. He's only lame on and off; he's sound to-day actually, but of course I shan't ride him."

We rode slowly home talking of lameness and horsy ailments. I learned a little from Christina about curbs and spavins.

Next day we jumped Clown at Bumpers over a bar lodged on two very low orange boxes, and he jumped very well, so well that we were heartened. Suddenly our way seemed clear. We had only to make him obedient to our hands and legs and—Philip Lockheed would add—our seat bones, and we would have an excellent all-round gymkhana pony and hunter. At last we began to realise that it is ordinary schooling on the flat—balancing exercises, suppling exercises, like the turn on the haunches and forehand, changes of rein at the trot and canter, circling to either hand at all paces, and the careful blending of extended and collected work—that eventually makes the perfect all-round mount. We began to understand that it is easy to keep a well-schooled pony straight at a fence, easy to place him and possible to help him, when necessary, to time the take off; whereas an unbalanced, untrained mount may be taught to get round a course of jumps or to perform in a potato race, but is likely to let his rider down or become difficult or nearly uncontrollable when frightened or upset. As Christina said, to ask a pony to bend properly in and out of posts at a canter before it has learned to lead off on the right leg, halt in a balanced manner and turn on the forehand, is like asking a child

115

to do decimals before it has learned to add up, divide or subtract.

We both felt that once Clown learned to respond to our aids willingly and automatically our difficulties would be over. To teach him to compete in gymkhana events and to jump would be simple.

And from that day onwards Clown seemed to improve, as though he had suddenly decided to cooperate.

I believe it is often like that with spoilt or difficult horses. For weeks the trainer toils without seeming to get anywhere, only keeping his temper with great effort and then, quite suddenly, a slight change comes over the horse; he decides to oblige and the trainer finds that all those weeks were not wasted; the horse did understand a little of what he tried to teach him and, now that he is co-operating, he learns twice as quickly.

I think that to ride a willing, supple and responsive horse is one of the most wonderful experiences. Clown seemed to have decided to develop all these qualities.

The memory of our disgraceful performance at the Chilswood Show filled us with determination to do better next time. The schooling of Clown became almost a crusade, and during the few days before the party we worked hard on him, harder than we had worked on any pony before. We gave him a large feed morning and evening and rode him for two hours each day, one hour was spent on intensive schooling in the field and the other hacking quietly through the woods, and up and down the steepest hills in the district.

The weather was perfect for riding: sunny, but with a cool breeze, which kept the flies away and prevented us from feeling lackadaisical. Waking each morning to find a beam of sunlight aslant my room, I looked forward to riding Daybreak and Clown; each night I went to bed heartened and filled with fresh hope.

"What can be more satisfying," I asked myself, "than to have a beautiful, lively and cheerful pupil who im-

116

proves during every moment of his lesson under one's very eyes?"

We were still in this gay and hopeful mood when Tuesday, August 10th, arrived. Although our guests were not going to ride, we thought they would like to see all the ponies, and we brought Daybreak and Clown to Hampton House for the day, turning Daybreak out in the field, where he neighed every five minutes with monotonous regularity.

Charlie was the first person to arrive; at twenty minutes past two, flapping her arms and legs, she came dashing up the drive on Jingle, who, as usual, wore a dirty bridle without a nose-band. She is the sort of child who always turns up at a party at the wrong time.

"I've lost Terry," she yelled, seeing us both standing by the stables. "He went off after a rabbit, but I expect he'll turn up soon. I say, we aren't going to play tennis, are we?—'cos I haven't brought my racket."

"Hallo! No, definitely not. Oh dear, we haven't left a box free for Jingle. Can he be turned out with Daybreak?" asked Christina.

"No fear! I don't want him kicked, thank you."

"Well, can we tie him up somewhere? To that fence? I hope Daddy won't mind," said Christina.

"Okeydoke," replied Charlie.

We had just settled Jingle when Phyllis arrived on foot, wearing a very clean flowered frock, which somehow seemed to make her droop even more than usual.

"I wanted to come on Swallow," she explained, "but he *wouldn't* be caught, and then I thought I should get so dirty riding, anyway; so I persuaded Daddy to give me a lift."

"You should never give in to a pony," said Charlie, who is a shocking rider.

"You're punctual to the tick," I said. "It's a pity you haven't a dog to bring."

"I don't like dogs much; they make everything so dreadfully dirty," said Phyllis, and at that moment

Shannan saw her and, remembering that his missis had once shared a tent with her, frolicked across the gravel and clawed her frock with his large muddy paws.

"Oh, get down, you naughty dog!" she implored.

"Fuss Pot," called Charlie.

"Shut up. Don't be rude to our guests," said Christina sharply, seizing Shannan by the collar and dragging him away from Phyllis.

"What a commotion," said Nigel, turning up the drive on Punch, with Gruffy, grunting like an old gentleman, at his heels.

From then until twenty to three our guests arrived in rapid succession. Piers was the only one who had refused out of all those to whom we had sent invitations. He was away. Presently there were thirteen of us on the lawn with six dogs. Apart from growing, my cousins had not changed much in appearance. They were still fair-haired, clean and very English. Their most striking, if not most attractive, features still struck me: Barbara's thick lips; Jill's snub nose; Stephen's chisel-like chin—as they had struck me two years before, when I was staying at my cousins' house, Tree Tops. I was curious to see whether they would agree well with Christina, because they, like her, are what Mummy calls prize-winning children.

It was awful at first. No one would talk. I introduced Tilly, who had not been at the camp, to Jill and they both said how do you do, and then turned away from one another. Then I introduced Charlie to Stephen and she said: "Oh, I say, you've come in a clean shirt. Didn't you see the invitation? You'll get terribly dirty."

And Terrence, who is eleven and bad-tempered, butted in and added: "Oh, boy, how swell!"

"Shut up," said Stephen, turning away as though to talk to Jill, who was standing looking at the ground.

"How are Sandy and Sunshine?" I asked. (They are my two youngest cousins' ponies.)

"Fine, thanks. Jill and Sunshine have been sweeping

the board this year—twenty rosettes and fifteen are firsts."

"What happened to High Jinks?" I asked; perhaps tactlessly, because my Aunt Margaret paid a huge sum for him and he turned out to be a thoroughly nasty pony.

"We sold him ages ago. *That* beastly animal will never be any good to any one," said Stephen emphatically.

"Mummy's going to buy me a first-class show hunter. He's got a superb front, faultless hocks, plenty of substance, a look of quality about him and he's a real daisy-cutter—will take some beating, I can tell you," said Jill, and her words reminded me of a horse-dealer's letter.

"Augusta," said Christina, "every one seems to want to see the ponies before we jump the dogs."

"Okay," I said.

I was curious to know what my three cousins would think of Christina's ponies, because in their part of the world Barbara, Stephen and Jill are believed to have a "good eye for a horse" and they certainly win a great many prizes, and are well informed in the theory as well as the practice of horsemanship.

"I want to take another look at the circus pony," said Nigel.

"How super! Has he really been in a circus? He seemed more like a bucking bronco at Chilswood," said Pat Folley.

"No, of course not. Nigel just invents things," Christina told her.

"Oh, I do *adore* Serenade," cried Charlie, flinging her arms round the bay pony's neck.

"Sloppy. Ponies don't like that—just like a girl," said Mike.

"He's Serenade, a part-bred Arab. I jump him, but he's a little bit lame at the moment, poor fellow," said Christina to Barbara, who replied:

"Oh, is he?"

"He's a lovely pony—such a sweet expression. I love to see you riding him," said Phyllis.

"Do you like him?" I asked Jill, opening the loosebox door so that she could see him better.

"Stands over at the knee," she answered shortly. Of course she was right, but I didn't like her for speaking the truth. Serenade has many good points; she could have so easily remarked on one of these, instead of picking on his only bad fault in conformation, for the sake of showing off how much she knew. If it had been the other way round—Christina looking at Sunshine—I'm quite sure Christina would have found something to praise in Jill's pony.

We passed on to Solo.

"He's nervous," said Christina, "but frightfully intelligent and quick. I just sit there in gymkhana events and he does it all. That is unless he takes it into his head to buck—then he chucks me off in front of every one."

"If he was a person he would wear specs," said Nigel.

"Oh *no*; he would be one of those very smart sprightly little men in shiny gaiters and coloured waistcoat—rather a nasty piece of work really," I contradicted.

"Nonsense; he would smoke a pipe and be domesticated," Nigel went on.

"He wouldn't," I said.

"Come on. Really, you can't start arguing about what a pony would be if it was a person—the thing's too much of a hypothesis," said Christina. "Don't you think it's a pity Solo's docked, Barbara?"

"It is, isn't it," Barbara answered.

"Bet he can turn on a sixpence," said Stephen.

"You're quite right, old chap, he can, but he's not so fast as my pony, Nightmare," said Mike.

"And here's Symphony," said Christina, patting the sleek chestnut neck.

"Do you like her?" I asked Jill, who paused before answering. "A trifle herring-gutted, I think. That's a fault my show hunter hasn't got, thank goodness."

"She's a silly horse—can't jump for nuts," said Charlie.

"She's not; she's sweet and so beautiful," said Phyllis.

"She's jolly nice, like a painting by Munnings—according to Piers," added Tilly.

"Golly, wasn't it a scream at the camp gymkhana when you fell off her?" said Pat Folley.

"I was disqualified for three refusals. At the last refusal I shot over her head. You know—one of those wonderful dives," Christina explained to my cousins.

"Did you really?" said Barbara.

I could have screamed at her then for being so dim and dull. I felt all my cousins needed a good shaking, or a firework let off behind them. While staying at Tree Tops I had not noticed their lack of conversation—here it was all too apparent.

"And now there's Clown. He's our pupil and a frightfully bad-mannered one, although *not* a circus pony," said Christina.

"He's sweet," said Phyllis, stroking Clown's pink nose, "but I think you're terribly brave to ride him. I wouldn't dare—not when he stands up on his hind legs."

"We all know you are a coward," said Mike spitefully.

"I think he's a jolly nice pony, so striking, and I love his markings," said Tilly.

It would have been easy for my cousins to say something, to ask how long we had had this new pony or whether he belonged to us. There was a score of openings; but they were silent.

"Do you think we can turn him into a good gymkhana pony?" I asked Jill.

"You can never cure rearers," she replied.

"I bet I could cure Clown if he was mine," said Terrence. "I would pull him over backwards or break a bottle on his head."

"Bet you wouldn't," said Charlie.

"Bet I would," contradicted Terrence.

"There's only Daybreak to see now," said Christina.

"Oh, you've still got old Daybreak then, Augusta," said Stephen.

"Oh yes, I shall never sell him. Actually he's not old —only reaching middle age," I said.

"You know him well, of course, don't you? I think he's a lovely ride, so gay and willing, don't you?" Christina asked Barbara, who answered:

"I suppose he is."

I decided then that my cousins must be frightened of Christina. In the field Daybreak was still neighing.

"He's a darling and he has such a sweet face too," said Phyllis.

"If he was a person he would wear plus-fours and play golf," said Nigel.

"What a lie! He *wouldn't*," I cried. "He's not gamey-fied at all. He's a most scholarly gentleman."

"Oh boy! a real toff with a butler and footmen like Christina," said Terrence.

"Shut up," said Mike, who seems to have become more friendly towards Christina lately.

"Let's jump the dogs now," I suggested.

Chapter 17 by Christina

OUR GARDEN has many paths most of which run between low, neatly clipped box-hedges; hedges which proved very useful on the day of the party, because we rested rakes and hoes, besoms and forks on them and so made a course of jumps for the dogs.

Augusta's cousins, three disappointingly dim children, did not help, but stood watching us disapprovingly—at least I thought they were disapproving, but they may be the sort of people who seem scornful when they are really feeling particularly shy and stupid. Anyway, we thought they might be bored and, as they had no canine friends, we asked them to judge the jumping and provided them with pencils and notebooks.

It was a very exciting competition. Tilly and Bandit, Pat and Rupert, and Augusta and Lucifer all achieved clear rounds. Shannan as usual behaved disgracefully and I became even more convinced that I was a hopeless dog-trainer. Although no jump was over two feet in height, he lay down and tried to crawl under each of them in turn, which, as you can imagine if you have seen many wolfhounds, made him look ridiculous. But in behaving so badly he did at least achieve one great feat—he brought a faint smile to the lips of Barbara and Jill.

Augusta looked anxious, as the course was raised for the jump off, and I knew that she did not want Lucifer to win because it was her party. But she need not have worried. He was very excited now and knocked down a besom and hoe; while Bandit, jumping with the precision of a clockwork mouse, timing each obstacle perfectly, and Rupert, both made clear rounds again. The two dogs, the spaniel and the terrier, went round the course once more and Bandit won. I gave Barbara one of Serenade's plain red rosettes and she awarded it to the terrier, and we all clapped, while Tilly tied it on to his collar.

"Piers *will* be pleased," she said.

And at that moment we heard a scream—a scream of horror and surprise, not terror. Mike, always quick in the uptake, was the first to move. "Someone in distress," he said dramatically and, leaping to his feet, he started running towards the lawn, from which direction the scream had come. The rest of us followed in his wake, the dogs yapping hysterically at our heels.

"Oh, I hope it's a murder!" cried Terrence.

"Bloodthirsty wretch," said Augusta.

"Probably only some children screaming in the road," I suggested.

In a very few moments we were on the lawn staring, not at a corpse, but at Shannan and Elsie, who acts as parlourmaid on Walters' day off, running round the two long tables on which tea had been laid. Between his long jaws Shannan held a large and once lovely chocolate cake. Elsie was flourishing a clean tea-towel. On the green, smooth turf lay the sad fragments of cups and saucers. Hearing our arrival, Elsie stopped.

"Oh, the naughty dog!" she cried. "I came out 'ere with a tray of trifles and what did I see?—but 'im gobbling up meringues; cream spurting out of 'is mouth, and china on the floor, and everything flying."

Mike tried to catch Shannan; while I, I'm sorry to say, stood rooted to the spot, aghast at the spectacle; Elsie with her cap on the ground, her hair on end, her eyes nearly popping out of her head; Shannan gallivanting round the tables, contriving to grin, crumbs of chocolate cake dropping from the corners of his mouth. To me it is an unforgettable scene. But while I stood, other minds were active. Suddenly, with a yap of joy,

Rupert, Rolly and Terry dashed at the gambolling wolfhound and tackled him low, and then, a moment later, the three other dogs joined in. Round the lawn the seven of them went, knocking over chairs, barking with wild delight, grabbing at each other's ears, while their owners called frantically, but in vain.

"I knew it would be a mistake to have dogs," Phyllis told Barbara.

"Gruffy will soon tire," said Nigel in sober and confident accents.

"Terry really *is* naughty!" exclaimed Charlie, giggling a little.

"Rupert has been properly trained, not like most spaniels of to-day, and he generally comes beautifully. It must be the other dogs' bad influence," said Pat, starting to call again.

"Rolly's the same," added Heather.

"Surely anybody, dog or human, who succumbs so easily to another's influence cannot be fairly described as well trained," remarked Nigel.

"Oh, don't be priggish," said Charlie.

"Shannan's only obedient when it suits him," I shouted, trying in vain to head and stop him.

Nigel was right. Gruffy soon tired and returned to his master, panting and snuffling in a pug-like manner, from the now wrestling throng. Presently Augusta caught Bandit and tied him to a tree, and then the rest of us managed to encircle and capture the remaining dogs and, ignoring their whines and pathetic glances, to tie them up in different parts of the garden. Returning to the lawn, Augusta, Tilly and I helped Elsie pick up the broken china and re-lay the table, and presently everything was rearranged and we had tea.

Augusta says it was a good tea, but I cannot agree. It seemed to me that there was too much food; it was overdone; it was like a display. The tables were laden. In addition to vast quantities of sandwiches, rock cakes and scones, there were meringues and éclairs simply oozing cream, cream and jam-filled sponge cakes, chocolate biscuits, sweet biscuits, shortbreads, trifles, jellies and ices. As I sat down, I felt my appetite fade away. Perhaps it was the heat which made me look at the tea-table with such disfavour, for the day had become very hot. The August sun shone from the bluest of blue skies and it seemed to burn right through my cotton frock and reach my bones. The air was very still; not a bough or leaf moved and the flowers drooped their heads in sad silence. Suddenly I wished that we had held the party at Bumpers, that Augusta and I had made the cakes and cut the sandwiches ourselves, and that our friends could have helped us wash up after tea. We might have climbed the trees in Augusta's orchard, too, I thought, and played with the bantams. It would have been much more interesting than sitting here in such orderly fashion. I became aware then that Charlie was speaking to me and that Terrence had an empty plate. I told every one to snatch what they wanted, and then asked Charlie to repeat what she had been saying. She asked me whether I honestly thought that Augusta and I could cure that brute, Clown. I said yes, certainly; he was getting much better, and Terrence, who—as I think Augusta has said before—has no manners—cried: "Oh yeah!"

"What do you mean by oh yeah?" I asked.

"Careful, Terrence; you are treading on dangerous ground," warned Nigel.

"I think you'll find that skewbald a difficult case," said Jill.

"Oh, do you? Have you had much experience with ponies of his sort of temperament?" I asked.

"Yes, I have, actually, and I warn you to be careful. They can give you some pretty nasty spills," said Jill with a knowledgeable air which irritated me.

"There you are!" said Terrence, "and *she* knows what's she's talking about."

"A little time ago you were boasting that *you* could cure Clown by breaking a bottle over his head. Now you agree with Jill that he is a very difficult case. It really seems most illogical to me," I said.

"Oh, *poor* little Christina. Well, you see, *you* wouldn't dare to break a bottle over his head. He needs a bronco buster, I expect."

For a moment I thought that I would ignore Terrence's mocking remark, and then the temptation became too great. Every one at my table was strangely quiet. Charlie's eyes were on my face. Heather's knife was poised in the air. Terrence's words suddenly became important; they became a challenge. I threw dignity to the winds.

"I would dare to do almost anything on Clown," I said, a little too hotly. "I wouldn't want to break a bottle over his head, because it would be cruel and unnecessary. He's nearly cured now; but I wouldn't mind riding him anywhere—into a river, into a shop, through Piccadilly."

"Bravely said!" cried Nigel.

"Oh yeah!" mocked Terrence.

I think if he hadn't been so small I really would have attacked him at that moment; instead I started to eat again.

"Well," said Terrence, "if you are so jolly brave and Clown's so perfect, I'll dare you to do something," he paused, thinking.

I wished that I had not boasted. I looked across to the other table to see if Augusta had heard the conversation; she was discussing apples with Tilly and Barbara, and eating a trifle. I noticed that the ices on my table were melting fast. They had been brought out too early. And I suggested that Jill might start on them.

Then Terrence said: "I dare you to jump Clown over one of these tables; like a horse in a book I once read."

I hate the daring habit, but I'm also foolish enough to hate refusing a challenge. I suppose I'm afraid of being thought a coward. I looked at the tables, which were less than three feet in height, eight feet long and about two feet three inches in width. I looked at the take off of smooth turf, at the run of sloping lawn and, in my imagination, I saw and felt Clown, as he gathered himself together to jump.

"All right, I'll accept the challenge. I think it's very silly though," I answered.

"Hurray!" cried Nigel, rising to his feet. "Ladies and gentlemen—no, correction—'Friends, Romans, Countrymen, lend me your ears.' To-day, at tea, while you have been thinking only of your stomachs, a challenge has been thrown out and accepted. In a few moments' time a steed of great beauty, once a circus pony, is to be jumped over this table." He paused.

"You sound very dramatic, but I haven't grasped what it is all about," said Augusta.

I explained.

"Oh, goodie! How exciting," cried Phyllis.

"I bet he jumps it beautifully," said Tilly.

"It's not exactly what I should ask a pony of his age and temper to do," said Jill.

"You're too cautious. That's why you don't win potato races," said Stephen.

"If you'll all finish tea, I'll fetch Clown," I told them, leaving the lawn at a brisk run. The sight of the intelligent skewbald head, looking earnestly over the loose-box door, filled me with sudden confidence. I felt that I had been a fool to grab Terrence's useless and idiotic bait, but I felt with equal certainty that Clown would jump the table. He nuzzled me gently, as I put the reins over his short little ears and, for the first time, I thought he was growing fond of me.

"You've got to do something very important," I said, "and you mustn't rear, not on any account." Then I remembered Ted Dunne's remark, *used to jump a bit too,* and the memory heartened me.

Before I took Clown to the lawn, I walked and trotted him in the drive, so that he should be wide awake when I asked him to jump the table. He obeyed my aids willingly and I felt even more confident. I was able to think quite calmly of what action I should take if he started to jib on the lawn. I was glad that my parents were out, because I realised suddenly that they would be angry if they knew that I was about to ride and leave hoofmarks on the so carefully tended green turf of Hampton House.

On arrival, I was greeted by cheers from Nigel, Tilly, Mike and Augusta and, to my surprise, they made me feel nervous, terribly nervous. My legs felt suddenly weak and my heart seemed to beat twice as fast as usual and I couldn't have eaten an ice if someone had offered me a pound to do it.

"Well, let's see if the circus pony knows any tricks," said Nigel.

"If you call rearing a trick, he certainly knows *one*," said Heather.

"I wish I had made it a bet instead of a dare," said Terrence.

"Now, Clown, your moment has come," whispered Augusta, giving him a lump of sugar. "Wouldn't it be best to keep him moving?" she added.

Jill seemed to be of the same opinion, for almost at the same moment she said: "Is it wise to keep a nappy youngster standing around eating sugar?"

The, possibly unintentional, scorn in her voice spurred me to action. All my confidence and determination of ten minutes ago returned. Charlie and Terrence watched me eagerly. Phyllis's face implored me to succeed. Barbara and Stephen looked despising but interested, as though the whole affair was rather childish and they were only watching because they happened to be on the spot. Tilly was tense, Nigel amused but cynical. Augusta—well I dared not look at her. In fact I looked at no one else. I said my thoughts aloud, "Now or never," and then trotted Clown across the lawn, delighting in his quick response and proud carriage. I turned and rested my eye for a second on the table, before looking at the turf in front and judging where we should take off. No one spoke; even the dogs, still tied in the garden, were silent. I felt that Time was standing still. And then I put him at the table; my eyes still on a small dent in the turf about three feet from it. Our lawn is not small, but the table was placed in the middle and so the run was short. I trotted a few yards, then pushed Clown on; he hesitated; I used my legs; and I believe that, if one can throw their heart over a jump, I threw my heart over that table.

"Go on!" said Augusta.

I used my legs again, so lengthening his stride and bringing us to the dent in the turf. And now he took off and instead of looking forward, as I should, I looked down and saw for a fleeting second the cutlery, the dirty china and the white tablecloth; and then we were over, and a cheer rang out from the spectators.

Then we were over

130

"He is *wonderful*," said Phyllis.

"What did I tell you?—a circus pony," added Nigel.

"He has improved," remarked Tilly.

"Not bad for a youngster," said Barbara.

"Jolly good. Well done, Clown," said Augusta, patting him about twenty times and giving him a shortbread. "I say," she continued, "those poor dogs; we must give them some tea. I really think we've been jolly mean—tying them up and leaving them. I bet they're thirsty. I'm going to fetch Lucifer. People, if your dogs would like it, please bring them here and we'll give them the remains of the cakes, milk and tea."

"You know, Christina, you needn't have taken what I said so seriously 'cos I was only teasing," said Terrence, screwing up his small sharp face as he spoke.

"Well, it's good for Clown to learn to jump tables," I answered; then, slowly with a glad heart, I led our skewbald pony back to his stable.

Chapter 18 by Augusta

AFTER CLOWN had jumped the table, our guests became suddenly more talkative. Jill conversed with Christina on the better-known show riders and horses, and as both of them had been to Dublin and competed in most of England's largest shows, they had much in common. Stephen and Mike wrestled with each other, and the rest of us played Hide and Seek and Release, until seven o'clock, when it was time to see two of Mr. Carr's films—The Riding Club Gymkhana and The Teddington Show; the first of which we enjoyed the most, because, except for Tilly and my cousins, we were all in it somewhere, and it was very interesting for us to see our faults. I noticed that I never had my weight in my stirrups while jumping, and Nigel realised, at last, that he generally rides with his toes down. Christina, of course, was the star and looked very smart, and I looked better than usual, because I was wearing one of her coats.

After Mr. Carr had shown us the films, we left the dining-room and went up to the nursery, where the large table was laid with plates of sardines on toast, lobster and oyster patties and other such eatables as, I believe, grown-ups eat at cocktail parties.

We brought the dogs with us. Once again they had been tied up, mostly to banisters, and they had been making a terrific noise. We gave them each an eatable and those who knew tricks performed. Gruffy, I remember, was very clever; he "read the lesson," prayed and walked on his hind legs, in addition to shaking hands, dying for King and Country and begging with indescribable dignity.

At nine o'clock sharp our guests' parents began to arrive and Elsie tramped upstairs to announce their names. Aunt Margaret, loud-voiced, full of horsy conversation, was the last. She had spent the afternoon and evening with Mummy at Bumpers. She admired Shannan—as she admires every pedigree and well-made animal—shook hands with Christina, gave me a vague pat on the shoulder and then left, with my cousins in tow. The room seemed very empty when all the people and dogs had gone.

"I wonder—are they hard-boiled or do they suffer from inferiority complexes? I mean Barbara and Jill —not so much Stephen?" said Christina.

"Just hard-boiled, I think," I replied heartlessly.

We talked a little about our party, and then Christina helped me saddle and bridle Daybreak and I departed with Lucifer in the gathering darkness to ride slowly and thoughtfully home.

The next day we lunged Clown, giving him about ten minutes' work at the canter. He behaved like an angel and never failed to lead off with the inside leg. We lunged him over a thick pole on the ground at the walk and trot and, towards the end of the lesson, he jumped over a pole resting on two teak buckets, without hesitation.

We took Clown back to the stable and rewarded him for his good behaviour with a double handful of oats, before riding him for an hour in the field, where we concentrated mostly on work at the walk and trot, the turn on the forehand and the rein-back—the last of which we had not taught him previously because we were afraid it might encourage him to get behind the bit or, worse still, to rear. We each schooled Clown for half an hour, taking it in turns to criticise each other's riding.

After lunch I rode Daybreak, and Christina Solo and Symphony, and a card arrived announcing that our riding club was holding an instructional rally in under three weeks' time; and the next day we went to a very large show in a very sumptuous horse-box, for which Mr. Carr paid all expenses. There were no gymkhana events and I only competed in the children's jumping. Daybreak was marvellous; the course was stiff and terribly smart. I rode badly and we made six faults, which gained us sixth place. Serenade was still lame and had to be left at home with Solo, so Christina only had Symphony, who won the pony class and a championship, which satisfied Mr. and Mrs. Carr.

Christina and I insisted on travelling back with the ponies and, as it was a thirty-mile journey and we sang all the way, we were both hoarse when the box eventually turned up through the imposing gates of Hampton House.

On the day following the horse show we again lunged Clown, raising the pole about four inches by putting bricks on the teak buckets. The fact that he had jumped the table so well had made us cautious; the thought that we were entrusted with a very talented pony—perhaps an Olympia winner—gave us an unfamiliar sense of responsibility. We decided that if he did not become a brilliant performer, we would be to blame; and we were determined not to overface or overjump him.

"Slow but sure," said Christina, and "Better safe than sorry," said I priggishly.

We continued lunging Clown, because we believed that lunging flexes the young horse's ribs and neck, and forces him to use his quarters, and brings his hindlegs under him. One of my favourite and most instructive and useful books describes lunging as: "The most complete Swedish gymnastics that we can give a horse." Needless to say, we spent some time nearly every day reading Christina's and my books on schooling and riding.

After lunging Clown for about a quarter of an hour, we took him and Solo for a long ride, losing ourselves for several hours in some vast beech-woods and not arriving back at Bumpers until darkness was obscuring the landscape.

The next day we schooled Clown and Solo for half an hour, and hacked Serenade and Daybreak. And so, in this way, the days passed with startling rapidity. Completely absorbed by the art of horsemanship, we hardly noticed what else went on around us and neither bathed nor played tennis. Our parents accused us of becoming narrow-minded and forbade us to mention "horse" in their hearing.

"You must be careful, Augusta, that you don't become a bore," said Mummy. "Horsy bores are, I think sometimes, the worst of all bores."

"It's always *Clown* now—*Clown* did this, *Clown* did that. Do you think *Clown* ought to have a rise to-day? Really, darling, do talk about something else sometimes," said Mrs. Carr.

She was a little unfair, actually, because we did not forsake our other ponies; we spoke of them too, and Christina fussed about Serenade's splint, which was still causing him to go lame every now and then.

Suddenly, the Carrs upset Christina and me by starting to plan a seaside holiday; not just a short one; that would have been all right; but a three weeks' holiday. It was sad news for me, because it meant that I should have to school Clown alone, but to Christina it seemed worse than sad; it was, according to her, intolerable and she was certain that they were hoping it would take her mind off riding.

"A holiday abroad—that would be different; but who wants to spend three whole weeks at Solworth-on-Sea, when they might be at home schooling three ponies?" she asked me.

"No one in their senses," I replied. "Clown is sure to go back and get bad habits again, while you're away."

"I don't think that, but I do want to stay and help make him really good. After all, we may not have much longer. Mr. Dunne may turn up any day now and say he wants him back or has found a home for him," said Christina.

Our talking was of no avail. Mr. and Mrs. Carr ordered rooms in an expensive hotel, which meant that Shannan must stay at home, but, as you will find out if you read on, Christina and I need not have worried for by the end of the month our pupil was in another's hands.

When Tuesday came round for the second time since our party, Tilly rang me up and asked us to come over to tea on Thursday and see her new bantam chicks. She told me that Seaspray was off her food, so she did not know whether she would be able to come half-way and meet us or not. I accepted the invitation, little knowing how sad a sight was to meet our eyes in Waywards Hollow on that gusty August day.

Chapter 19 by Christina

WEDNESDAY DAWNED fair and warm. Walking down
the garden path in the young sunlight at nine o'clock
to see my ponies, I looked forward to jumping Clown
at Bumpers, and was unpleasantly surprised to see Ted
Dunne standing by the stables. My first impulse was to
run away and hide, but I forced myself to walk on and
call out "good morning."

"Good morning, Miss. I've come about that pony of
mine. 'Ow's 'e getting on?"

I hesitated. If I spoke the truth, telling him that
Clown seemed cured, would he take him away? I
asked myself. Should I say Clown still reared occasionally, that he needed another month's schooling and a
bit of cub-hunting, before he could be described as
safe? Best to be completely honest, I decided.

"He's improving a lot; he hasn't reared since the
Chilswood Show and he's jumping two feet six quite
nicely and has lost all his nervousness, but he still
needs careful handling," I said.

"Well done! Would 'e suit a little girl, do you think?
I know of one, about twelve or thirteen, who wants a
nice sort of pony with a bit of life about it. Would
'e suit 'er like?"

"He might with a bit more schooling, but it depends
how well the girl can ride," I replied.

"Oh, she's a good little 'orsewoman—often comes
trotting past my place on 'er own little roan, but she's
got too big for it, too 'eavy really."

I pictured a large child in wellington boots tearing
along the road on a small, fat, unkempt pony.

"I wonder why she doesn't belong to our riding club," I said.

"It's like this, Miss. I've got to get rid of the pony. Neither you or I want to keep 'im through the winter, so it seems that, as there's an 'ome going now, I might just as well sell 'im now. The girl's seen you and your friend riding 'im and 'as taken a fancy to 'im like."

"We've grown very fond of Clown, but certainly our parents don't want us to have him for good. I should think the girl had better come over here and try him," I said sadly.

"Where's the pony now? Can I see 'im?"

"He's at my friend, August's place, Bumpers. I've arranged to ride him there this morning."

"Are you going there soon? I've got the old car. I could run you round, if you like," offered Ted Dunne.

"Thanks awfully; that'll be fine, if you're sure you don't mind. Can you wait a sec.? I must just dash in and fetch my coat."

Indoors, I told my parents where I was going and rang up Augusta.

"Ted Dunne's coming to see Clown in a few moments. Do you think you can possibly catch and groom him?" I said.

"Oh gosh! how awful. Wait a minute; let me collect my wits. Clown's in the stable now and actually I *have* groomed him, but I'll do him again. Ted Dunne isn't going to take the poor fellow away, is he?"

"He's found a home for him, but what can we do? We can't buy him ourselves. I must dash—see you in a moment," I answered before ringing off.

All the way over to Bumpers my heart sank lower and lower, and the worst of it was that I knew there was no escape. Clown had got to go. I could not expect my parents to keep another pony for me and Augusta's parents certainly could not afford to buy him. I pictured Clown being ridden by the girl in wellington boots; his mane long and muddy; his bridle without a nose-band. I pictured him in the show ring, refusing

138

three times at the first jump in the children's jumping; and I pictured him rearing and plunging in the hunting field. If only he was going to be sold to someone I knew, it wouldn't be so bad, I told myself, someone who gave the same aids, used the same methods as Augusta and I.

I expect Ted Dunne thought I was mentally deficient, for I hardly answered his many questions and then in the most vague and abstracted way. His car rattled and clanked and smelt strongly of petrol. The road to Bumpers is very rough, and by the time we arrived I was feeling quite sick.

Augusta hurried us round to the stable. Clown was looking superb. The beauty of his head, his kind brown eyes, delicately cut ears, fine tapering nose struck me as they had never struck me before. He was like china, a lovely brown and white Dresden horse. As we approached he gave a low welcoming whinney. I felt a knot rise in my throat; I swallowed hard and told myself not to be a dog in the manger. Augusta was speaking.

"No, he's lost all his old nervousness, but he'll never be suitable for a beginner. He really wants to go to a fairly experienced girl, who'll ride him in gymkhanas and hunt. He's wasted anywhere else."

"This little girl I'm thinking of—she rides quite well, plucky like, and 'er father's willing to give a nice bit for the pony. 'E's quite a wealthy man, so they say, and I 'ope you'll accept a bit—seeing that you've put so much work into the pony."

"Oh, we don't mind about that; it's been a pleasure, thank you. We are only anxious that Clown should have a really suitable home."

"Yes, that's the main thing," I echoed.

" 'E's looking well and no mistake. Gave you a ride at Chilswood, didn't 'e?" asked Ted Dunne with a laugh.

"He certainly did. I think the loudspeaker frightened

him. Would you like to see him ridden now?" said Augusta.

"If you've got a moment to spare, Miss."

Clown behaved faultlessly. The day was gusty; leaves rustled; boughs creaked; a few early apples fell to the ground; but he did not seem to notice these little noises, which might have distracted many another pony. He seemed to give all his attention to his rider; every aid he obeyed instantly. I half hoped that he would nap, jib as he was about to pass the garden gate, but no thought of such an action seemed to enter his mind. As the phrase goes, Augusta had him "between her hands and legs." We had started schooling him in a double bridle a few days before, and now, as Ted Dunne stood and watched, he started to collect, quite naturally, without any fuss. He cantered on either leg, circled at all places —flexing his neck and ribs at last, like a trained pony —back reined, stood quite still to be mounted and jumped over two hen coops—placed back to back.

"Well done, Miss," said Ted Dunne. "I wouldn't recognise 'im as the same pony, that I wouldn't."

"He's marvellous," said Augusta, dismounting. "So obliging, so clever and so sweet. We'll miss him terribly."

"Can the little girl come and try him tomorrow?" asked Ted Dunne.

"Let's see. We are going to tea with Tilly in the afternoon, aren't we, August? The morning would be all right though, wouldn't it?" I said.

"Well, I'll call in like on my way back and see 'er father—Trenchard's the name, Major Trenchard— quite a nice gentleman. If 'e says that's all right, I won't do anything, see? But if 'e can't make it the morning, I'll let you know. Only the girl's in an 'urry, looking forward to getting a new pony and all," explained Ted Dunne.

"About eleven would suit us best," said Augusta.

"All right, Miss."

When Ted Dunne had left, we stood looking at Clown.

"Of course, we knew this had to happen in the end," I said.

"I could never be a horse-dealer," said Augusta.

"It's awful, isn't it, and we've grown so fond of him."

"It would be different if he was going to someone we knew and liked."

"You wouldn't like him to be sold to Charlie or Terrence, though," I told her.

"No, but I shouldn't mind so much if Jill bought him, or even the Folleys or Tony Allbright. At least we would know how he was getting on and hear if he suddenly turned vicious and was about to be sold for dog's meat."

"Yes, that's true. But let's stop talking about it. The plucky little girl may turn out to be awfully nice, and then we will have wasted an awful lot of a lovely day worrying unnecessarily," I said.

"I suggest we go for a beautiful long ride, then, and don't mention Ted Dunne, or Clown's future, once," said Augusta.

"Righto," I agreed.

But, of course, we broke our good resolution; we could not keep our minds off the fate of our pupil, and when we returned to Bumpers at half-past twelve the birds were singing, the baker's boy was whistling, Martha was humming, but we were sunk in the deepest gloom.

Chapter 20 by Augusta

IN APPEARANCE, Major Trenchard was not as we had expected; small, dark, unassuming and insignificant, he did not seem like a military man; and his daughter surprised us, too, for she was very small and pale, with fair, thin hair, pale blue eyes and protruding teeth. As Christina said afterwards, one could not possibly imagine Pauline Trenchard riding in wellington boots.

After Christina had ridden Clown around the orchard at the walk, trot and canter, and jumped him over two of my hen coops, I asked Pauline if she would like to have a ride, and she whispered "Yes, please," and cautiously stroked Clown's nose. Major Trenchard legged her up, and as soon as she was in the saddle I began to feel apprehensive. She looked stiff and very white-faced and nervous.

"You have ridden quite a lot before, haven't you? You'll find he likes rather a loose rein and answers to very light leg aids—a *squeeze*," said Christina, adjusting the stirrups.

"Yes, he's lovely," whispered Pauline.

"She fell in love with him quite a long time ago. She watched you lunging him at Hampton House, from the other side of the fence," said Major Trenchard.

"Oh, really," said Christina.

"He's just like a circus pony," whispered Pauline.

"Okay, your stirrups are all right now," I said, wishing that she would relax her desperate grip on the reins.

"There you are, Pauline. Ride him round," said Major Trenchard, adding when his daughter was out of earshot: "She takes a long time to get used to a pony; she's as happy as anything on her own Lassie, dare everything with her."

In spite of Christina's advice, Pauline had sent Clown into a walk with a quick, nervous kick with both heels; and now, each moment as I watched her riding, my apprehension grew, and with it, unwanted and useless, grew hope. If Pauline did not like Clown we could keep him a little longer; we could, perhaps, find a special and suitable home for him. I watched the pony and rider with great concentration. I did not hear Major Trenchard's remarks nor Christina's replies, but I saw Clown's lost expression, how he looked back at Pauline with distressed, uncertain eyes, and the longer I looked the more I seemed to love and admire Clown; the more tragic seemed the parting, which must come in the end. It was obvious that he did not understand his rider; her little jerks at his mouth and timid kicks conveyed no signal to his mind, but he was trying to oblige, to do the right thing; and I marvelled at his quietness. I remembered the distraught, nervous, stubborn pony which had arrived at Hampton House over seven weeks ago; I remembered the fight at the end of Foxey Lane and my own mad gallop round the ring at Chilswood; and for a moment I felt a tremendous sense of satisfaction and then it had gone; it had been replaced by a feeling of disappointment. I hoped now that Clown would misbehave, that he would have a fit of temperament and chuck Pauline into a soft bed of long grass; but I hoped in vain. He was nervous and very careful; he seemed afraid that his rider might fall off and he moved with the utmost caution.

"Quiet enough, isn't he?" remarked Major Trenchard.

"Yes, nearly always now, but you can't quite rely on him; he's rather a peculiar character, I think," answered Christina.

"You never know what is going to frighten him," I

added, thinking: oh dear, he's going on his forehand and he's behind the bit, too.

Pauline cantered Clown for a few yards and then, after riding round at the walk for what seemed like an age, came back to us, dismounted and whispered: "He's lovely, Daddy, but I'm not quite sure if I can stop him."

For a moment I felt hope return; then it was dashed to the ground.

"I shouldn't worry about that. If you feel perfectly happy about everything else, we'll have the pony," said Major Trenchard firmly.

I watched Pauline's pale face. I looked at her sticking-out teeth and I longed for her rabbit mouth to open and say, "I shall never be able to control him." But seconds, which seemed like minutes, passed and she did not speak. I glanced at Clown, as he stood—so handsome and intelligent—beside Christina. I did not know myself whether he would suit Pauline. I all but said that I thought he would not. I was only stopped by the not unfamiliar pricking of my conscience.

"Are you happy about everything else?" asked Major Trenchard patiently, and Pauline whispered something to him that we could not hear, and then he said. "Well, if you don't mind, I think I had better talk the matter over with my wife. Can I ring you up in a day or two?"

We said "Yes, certainly," and "That'll be fine," and as the Trenchards stepped into their car to leave, Christina said: "If Pauline is at all nervous, I don't think Clown is suitable."

The Major replied that she would soon get used to him, and presently they had gone and we ran indoors to tell Mummy what had happened.

All the way to Waywards Hollow, Christina and I discussed the Trenchards and Clown; and our ponies, realising our inattentiveness to themselves, picked leaves, dawdled and made disagreeable faces at each other. We forgot that Tilly might be meeting us half-way, that Seaspray had been off her feed; and we were horrified when we arrived and found Tilly sitting on the doorstep of the pink cottage with her head in her hands.

"Hallo, what's up?" I called.

"You look in the last stages of despair," added Christina.

"I am," said Tilly in a broken voice.

"Can we help?" I asked, standing at the garden gate.

"Nobody can help, nobody at all," answered Tilly, starting to cry.

"Do tell us what's the matter?" said Christina.

"Would you rather we went away?" I asked.

"Go into the stable and you'll see what's wrong. *Go* on. Don't stand here staring. You know the way, don't you?"

"All right," I said.

We took our ponies into the little paddock. "It must be Seaspray," I said. "You go first. I'il hold Daybreak and Symphony," offered Christina. I handed her my reins and walked to the loose-box; the top door was open; I looked over the bottom one and the sight which met my eyes is something I shall never forget; even now as I write I can recall it as though it was only yesterday that it happened. Seaspray was there standing in the far corner, but she was scarcely recognisable; her dear grey face was pinched and drawn; her eyes were sunken, her nostrils dilated and her mouth closed; her soft grey nose was poked out; her back was hollowed and her tail raised. She stood with heaving flanks, outstretched limbs and with such an expression of terror, as I had never seen on any animal's face before. For a minute I could hardly believe my eyes. One reads terrible descriptions of diseases and injuries, one is told horrible stories of pain and suffering, but although one feels horror and sadness, I do not think one often imagines it happening to one's own animals or relatives. It seemed incredible, almost impossible, now that this pony could be Seaspray, the Lockewoods' gay, clever little grey mare. Why should she, the most blameless of characters, be struck by this cruel disease? —if disease it was—I asked myself. She was not my pony, but I had always admired and loved her and I felt ready to cry. "Seaspray, poor little Seaspray," I said softly, but not softly enough. She had not been aware of my presence and the sound of my voice startled her. She tried to move, but her contracted muscles were too stiff and rigid; and she showed the haws of eyes, and then she had the most awful spasm, and with a cry I ran to Christina.

"Oh, it's terrible, horrible. Poor, poor Seaspray— oh, poor Tilly," I gasped.

"Take the reins," said Christina, and the next moment she had gone and I was holding the two ponies. She stayed looking over the loose-box door for an age —or so it seemed to me—and I patted Daybreak and remembered Seaspray jumping, Seaspray hunting; Seaspray at the camp, whinneying when her breakfast was brought, standing patiently while her socks were washed, watching Piers with her soft brown eyes. At last Christina returned.

"What do you think it is?" I asked.

"Lockjaw," she replied.

"Or it can be called Tetanus, can't it? I believe you are right. I remember a picture in one of my veterinary books. Oh dear, the pony there stood just like Seaspray is standing." The knot in my throat tightened as I spoke.

"The symptoms in the book were the same too, I think," said Christina in a very quiet, calm voice.

My eyes began to water and then I felt tears and I hid my face in Daybreak's lovely warm mane. Presently Mrs. Lockewood came into the paddock and sadly explained to us what had happened. She said Seaspray *was* suffering from tetanus and the vet had no hope. He had injected her and would continue to inject her as long as she lived, but very few horses survived such an acute attack. After some search a small deep puncture had been found in her coronet, through which the germ must have entered.

"If we had known of the wound's existence before, we might have averted all. I do not think we would have had the sense to have her injected against tetanus, but at least we would have kept the place clean and probably washed out with antiseptic, what the vet describes as 'the pus and soil, which favour the development of the micro-organisms of tetanus.' "

I did not entirely understand the explanation, but I was silent, because I could not control my voice. I swore to myself that if ever any horse of mine was pricked by the blacksmith or had any deep wound or puncture, I should follow the advice of my veterinary books and have him injected against tetanus.

We asked Mrs. Lockewood if there was anything that we could do to help Tilly or Seaspray, and she thanked us and said she could not think of anything. Tilly did not want to speak to any one and the busier she was kept the better. Seaspray could not eat and, if she did not show improvement soon, would have to be destroyed. The last word, mentioned with—probably unintentional—casualness by Mrs. Lockewood, made my heart feel like lead, and it needed all my strength to get myself up into my saddle. It was obvious that we were neither wanted nor expected to stay to tea, nor had we any wish to stay.

With sad thoughts we took a miserable farewell and set our ponies' heads for home, and they, unaware of any tragedy, walked with gay carriage and long easy strides.

"It must be terrible for Tilly, because if only she had noticed the puncture and kept it clean, all might have been well," I said.

"O'Neil would have insisted on an anti-tetanus injection at once," added Christina.

"She must be terribly haunted by remorse, and how awful to have to explain everything to Piers," I said with a shudder.

147

"Seaspray was such a gay, willing pony, too. You couldn't help loving her. She always reminded me of Dobbin, my first rocking-horse," said Christina.

It was only when we were nearly home that we thought of Clown again.

"You know we ought to have made a special plan of action. I can't think how we could have been so silly and vague over such an important thing. That girl didn't try him for nearly long enough. She should have groomed and saddled and bridled him, and taken him out on the road. I don't think it's fair or sensible that a pony should be sold with so little trial," said Christina.

"We certainly were jolly feeble. I'm afraid I thought, 'Fate will decide,' which was perfectly idiotic. But I'm not sure that Clown wouldn't be happy with Pauline. She wouldn't knock him about anyway and we would see him. I don't know; I suppose she would be too timid and, although he behaved well with her to-day, he would soon deteriorate if she rode him often. Couldn't we arrange, with Dunne's approval, for the Trenchards to have Clown on a week's trial?" I suggested.

"Yes, that's an idea. If they ring up and say they want him, let's suggest it. But perhaps they will decide that he's quite unsuitable. Wouldn't it be wonderful if they did?" said Christina hopefully.

Chapter 21 *by Christina*

ON FRIDAY we exercised Clown and schooled Daybreak and Symphony, in preparation for the riding club rally, for three-quarters of an hour; and in the evening I rang up Waywards 21 to inquire after Seaspray with a feeling of intense dread. Mrs. Lockewood answered the telephone; always brusque, she seemed even more brusque than usual this evening and I wondered whether I was sounding irritatingly inquisitive or being a tiresome nuisance. Then I heard the awful news.

"It's over," she said. "Seaspray died early yesterday morning."

"Oh!" I exclaimed. "Oh, I *am* sorry—how terrible!" And then my voice petered out; I could think of no adequate words. I felt quite weak, so shocked that I might just as well not have known that the pony's life had been in danger.

"I'm making Tilly go to the riding club thing to-morrow. It'll do her more good than being miserable at home. I expect you'll see her there. Thank you for ringing up. Good-bye," said Mrs. Lockewood and rang off.

Augusta was disagreeably surprised and shocked too. We talked about Tilly and Seaspray all the way to the rally, which was being held at Eleanor's place, the next morning, and I could not banish the sight of the grey mare's pinched, suffering face from my mind. I led Clown from Daybreak. The Trenchards had not rung us up—a fact that filled us with hope—and we could not resist taking him for Eleanor to see; we had arranged with her that he should be shut in a loose-box during most of the rally.

Tilly arrived at a quarter to eleven, and very soon we began to wish that she had not come. The other club members were unintentionally brutal; they had not heard of the tragedy and they asked again and again why Seaspray was not present, and you can well imagine Tilly's difficulty in replying. Eleanor, Augusta and I tried to warn them as they arrived, but without much success. Tilly alone was unmounted, an unusual state of affairs.

Suddenly Augusta had a brainwave. "I've got an idea. I can't think why we didn't think of it before. Let's lend Clown to Tilly," she said.

"Will she be able to manage him?" I asked dubiously.

"If I can, she can," answered Augusta firmly.

We fetched Eleanor and she agreed it was a good suggestion. And so, at eleven o'clock, the rally began, taken by a well-known equitation expert called Colonel Windham, a tall, lanky, clean-shaven man, who wore a brown homburg and coat, fawn breeches and well-fitting brown boots; and Tilly, looking very nice and competent, rode Clown, and everybody who had made tactless remarks began to feel better.

I was the first in the class to be corrected; intent on watching Tilly and her mount, I forgot to keep a length's distance between Symphony and the pony in front, and was sharply rebuked. We schooled for nearly an hour, finishing with half passes at the trot for Augusta, Pat, Tony Allbright and myself, which was very interesting and very instructive. Terrence was rather a blot, because he would try to play the fool and, odd though it may seem, Colonel Windham did not seem very good at keeping order—but perhaps he did not think Terrence worth bothering about. Clown went beautifully. Tilly kept her hands almost completely still and he dropped his nose like a dressage horse. Excited by the other ponies, lively and gay by

He dropped his nose like a dressage horse

nature, he seemed to collect himself; and I do not believe any other animal there moved with such grace and carriage.

When we finished schooling, we jumped; and again Clown went well. Tilly did not put him at anything higher than two feet six, but he approached each fence as though he loved jumping. At lunch-time Colonel Windham asked Tilly if she owned Clown and she told him about Ted Dunne and about our breaking and schooling efforts, and the tea table. Presently he came across to Augusta and I and, after admiring Daybreak and Symphony, said that we were making a very good job of the skewbald and that the little dark girl rode well.

After lunch Eleanor arranged gymkhana events— bending, potato and relay races. She agreed with us that to compete in these events, at his present stage of schooling, would only do Clown harm; so Tilly helped judge and stick up bending poles. Colonel Windham had gone home, but Eleanor corrected outstanding faults in our riding, and at three o'clock gave us all a lesson in rugging and bandaging. Tilly disappeared and we found her patting Clown in the stable.

"He's lovely," she said, "so good and obliging; he's like poetry to ride."

"I think you managed him jolly well," said Mike.

"You looked awfully nice on him, just the right size; and I think Christina and Augusta ought to be congratulated on their schooling, especially after all the unkind things that have been said about them."

These words of Phyllis's made me curl up inside; while Augusta said "Nonsense."

Mrs. Lockewood arrived in her car to fetch Tilly a few moments later, and she, too, admired Clown.

But it was only on the way home that Augusta and I suddenly realised the obvious solution to our problem.

"Somehow," said Augusta, "we must see that Clown is sold to Tilly. It would be the perfect home for him.

152

She is small and light and probably would never grow out of him."

"Can the Lockewoods afford to buy him, though? —that's the point," I said.

"We don't know how much Ted Dunne is asking for him," Augusta reminded me.

"No, but remember he hinted that he would give us a bit, a fiver or something. We could find out his price and then knock that off."

"I wonder if the Trenchards have come to any decision. The more I think about Pauline the more unsuitable she seems for Clown. We were fools not to put them off in the very beginning," said Augusta.

"Have you got anything you can sell to help buy him?" I asked.

"No, I don't think so. I had to pawn to buy Daybreak, you know; but a lot of my things were shut away in store, then. I'll think," promised Augusta.

"I've got a doll's house and a tennis racket, and perhaps Mummy will let me sell a piece of jewellery," I said, racking my brain.

"We must find out if Tilly and her mother want Clown first. We've got to be most awfully tactful," said Augusta.

As we rode back through the beechwoods, along broad leafy tracks where the sun threw sudden gleams of gold and the air smelled of earth, and wood, and leaves, and past dampness, we thought deeply on this subject.

Once home, Augusta turned Daybreak out with a feed in one of our fields and helped me choose what to sell of my belongings. The doll's house, which Daddy had bought me at vast expense some eight years ago, we decided was worth about five pounds.

A bracelet, for which my hand and wrist had grown too big, we guessed might fetch two pounds; and a gold watch which Mummy won't let me wear because she's afraid I'll lose it, we reckoned was worth twenty pounds. Augusta was worried because she could not think of anything to sell herself. "I don't seem to have any possessions at all," she said.

At tea I told my parents of our plans, and Mummy gave a cry of horror. "Darling," she said, "you are *not* going to sell that watch. I won't let you wear it now because you *will* tear around doing such silly things; but when you are older and more sensible and are going to balls and cocktail parties, you will be very glad of it. Really, I don't know what Aunt Denise would say, if she heard you were swopping the beautiful watch she gave you for a pony. I'm beginning to wish now that your father had never bought you all these animals."

"But surely, Mummy, ponies are more important than mere man-made things. I mean they're alive; they feel; they've got hearts and souls. A watch doesn't care if it changes hands," I said.

"Christina, you are *not* going to sell that watch, and what I say is final."

"Then we won't be able to buy Clown for Tilly and he'll go to a beastly home and finish up at the slaughter-house."

"Don't most horses finish up at the slaughter-house or kennels? Really, Christina, I think you are being rather silly. If Mrs. Lockewood wants Tilly to have Clown she'll let you know. If she doesn't want him, what is the use of you trying to buy him for her. I'm not going to keep the pony here indefinitely; three are enough; and the Thornedykes don't want to feed him through the winter; so why not wait and see what happens before you start making mad plans and offending your aunt and mother?" asked Daddy.

"Then, before we know where we are, the Trenchards will have bought him, and I'm sure he won't like Pauline. You haven't seen her; you don't know how unsuitable she is—pale, weak and fragile with sticking-out teeth," I said.

"Well, the Lockewood girl always looks pretty fragile to me," retorted Daddy.

"But she's not nervous and she can ride. She proved that this morning," said Augusta.

"She let her last pony die of tetanus," replied Daddy.

"That was bad luck. She didn't know that Seaspray was cut at all, nor did she know that the tetanus germ enters through wounds. It might happen to almost any one, I should think," said Augusta.

"I'm quite sure that she'll be a most cautious and careful owner now," I added. "It must be terrible for her to realise that, if she had been more careful and looked Seaspray over every day, as the experts say you should, the pony might still be alive. And then she'll remember a rigid, little grey mare with outstretched limbs and a suffering expression and be haunted by remorse; and think how awful that'll be. Whereas, if she has Clown, she might forget about it."

"Your reasoning is not very coherent. It seems to me that you've suddenly become very sentimental and imaginative," remarked Daddy.

"I'm sorry. I didn't mean to offend Denise—Aunt Denise. I won't sell the watch. I'll think of something else instead," I told my parents, because it is no good arguing with grown-ups.

The subject was dropped and we talked about gardens and flowers and, later, the seaside holiday, which I was dreading.

Chapter 22 by Augusta

"IT'S AWFUL, isn't it? I hate parting with all these old friends," I said.

"Oh, August! Surely you can't mind about a few dusty candlesticks and pieces of silver," said Christina incredulously, before adding in virtuous tones: "Anyway, Clown's worth the sacrifice."

"Without doubt," I answered.

We were standing outside Bumpers looking at a pathetic collection of objects which were to be sold in aid of Clown. Christina has many possessions and she had soon gathered together twenty pounds' worth, which the Carrs' chauffeur had obligingly brought over to Bumpers. There was her imitation red brick doll's house, two children's tennis rackets, a silver bracelet, a modern pendant—only lately given to her by a godmother—a silver porridge bowl and an elegant dressing-case. In addition to these, she had ten pounds in Post Office Savings. What had I to compare with these riches? Mummy and I had searched Bumpers from top to bottom, and at the end of two hours had collected a few pitiful objects with which we could bear to part. Of these, the most valuable and the most cherished was a first edition of Stevenson's *Kidnapped*, which had belonged to different members of the family for a good many years and had been left to me by my grandmother. The other things were of small value—two brass candlesticks, an ugly silver sugar sifter, which had been a wedding present to my parents, four school story-books, given to me by my cousins, two photograph frames, a water-colour by an almost unknown artist, a stuffed rabbit, and a cup won by Daybreak at a gymkhana. After ransacking all the drawers in the house, I had found my savings' book, which revealed that I had one pound two and tuppence in the Post Office.

"My lot are not worth more than ten pounds in all, I'm afraid," I said.

"Well, that'll be enough," Christina told me. "When I rang up Mr. Dunne last night he was a little disappointed, because he had not heard from the Trenchards, and although he asked forty, when I suggested thirty from us and pointed out that we would not accept anything for the schooling, whatever happened, he jumped at the offer; so, if your things are really worth that, we are all right."

"Yes, with *Kidnapped* I'm sure they are," I replied, a little sadly, because I hated parting with the first edition and I knew that Mummy was sorry to lose it too.

"Now we know we can get enough money, we must ring up the Lockewoods," said Christina.

"That's going to be most frightfully difficult. Let's toss up to decide on whom shall fall the fearful task," I suggested.

"I think it's *your* job, because I had to manage Ted Dunne last night."

"Only because you agreed that I am hopeless at talking business and beating people down," I replied.

"Well, then, I'm hopeless at being tactful."

"All right; what do you want me to say?"

"I think you should talk as though Clown was already ours—he is really—and ask if Tilly would like to borrow him indefinitely. I don't think it's any good offering to give him to Tilly, because I don't think they would accept."

"We've got to decide, somehow, how we are going to sell all these objects," I said, looking again at *Kidnapped*. "I'll tell you what," I added suddenly, "I'll sell my watch instead of the first edition. It might fetch

157

three or four pounds, and if I take my money out of the Post Office as well I won't be far short. I could borrow some money from you and pay it back soon. I'll weed people's gardens and scrub floors. I'm awfully good at earning money."

"I don't think your watch is worth more than two pounds—I mean it's nothing at all special. But if you hate parting with the book, I'll lend you some and you needn't pay it back unless you want to," said Christina.

"Oh dear, isn't everything difficult. I wish Mummy would let me sell my wardrobe. Of course, I'm going to pay you back." As I spoke, the telephone bell rang. I answered it.

"Mrs. Lockewood speaking. Is that Augusta?"

"Yes, good morning." My heart started to beat furiously. Could this be good news?

"It's about Clown," she went on. "I tried to get Christina, but she's not at home. Do you two own the pony or does he belong to someone else still? The point is, that I should like to buy him, if possible, for Tilly, who's fallen for him completely; although she would never think of asking us to buy her anything and doesn't even know that such a plan is a-foot."

"Oh, good!" I said quite calmly, although my heart seemed to be pounding against my ribs and my hands were shaking, so that I could hardly hold the receiver. "I am glad. That's marvellous. Tilly gets on so well with him. Ted Dunne still owns him really, I suppose. We were half negotiating to buy him, because we wanted to be sure that he had a suitable home, but we would far rather you bought him for Tilly."

"Do you know what Mr. Dunne's price is?"

"Yes, thirty pounds—not guineas. I think it's reasonable," I replied, wondering how my voice managed to sound so matter of fact, while my mind seemed in such a turmoil.

"The pony is quite reliable now, isn't he?" asked Mrs. Lockewood.

"Yes, I think so. He hasn't reared or played up for a long time."

"Is this Mr. Dunne on the telephone? My husband is paying for Clown and I should like to get everything settled before he changes his mind—you never know with husbands."

Feeling that I could jump the moon at this moment, I gave her the details. As I left the telephone I saw—in my mind's eye—Clown with Tilly; out hunting first, then jumping in the show ring, and then grazing contentedly in the little paddock by the pink cottage, sheltered from the weather, hidden from the world by trees, warm friendly beech trees. And then I saw *Kidnapped*, restored to its shelf in my white bookcase; and I looked at my shabby, battered watch, with its dear scarred, familiar face, and was glad that I could keep them both.

A week later we went for a long hack together. Tilly rode Clown, Christina Symphony, and myself Daybreak. We took sandwiches and, breaking the law, bought cider at a little whitewashed inn which stood with its back to a green and wooded slope at the end of a fertile, sunlit valley. We were fortunate, for the weather could not have been more perfect. The day was warm, but not sultry; and few flies bothered us; and the air was wonderfully light. A little breeze fanned our faces and lifted Clown's fine skewbald mane, and, because it had rained during the night, the earth, the trees and the few late flowers smelled like heaven, as fresh as a spring day. Everywhere the farmers and their men seemed at work, cutting the high, ripe corn which so nearly matched Symphony in colour.

I do not think that there was anything unusual about that hack, but it has remained clear in my memory longer than many a more eventful ride. Perhaps it is because I was so pleased to see Clown happy, to look back and remember the early days when we were near despair, when O'Neil was slashing him with a whip

159

and my conscience was pricking me miserably, when Mrs. Carr was driving herself into a frenzy and Christina was trying to hide her cut fingers. And, with remembering, I felt a little pride; for here was the "vicious brute" a calm, well-mannered pony, doing his work with apparent pleasure, and sold, I hoped for life, to a suitable home where he would be truly appreciated.

Tilly, I knew, had not forgotten Seaspray. There were times when she was sad and silent; but Clown's gaiety could not leave her untouched, and I had not seen her so cheerful since her pony's death.

Christina was determined to enjoy the ride, because the following day the Carrs were leaving for the seaside and her ponies were to be turned out for three weeks. She told us that she was not dreading the holiday any more, now that Clown was happily sold. After leaving Tilly and her mount at Waywards Hollow, she and I rode back together, down the grassy track, eerie with evening shadows, through the great silent woods and out on to the main road; and, presently, the sun set in a glory of crimson and gold, and we agreed that next year we must find another pony to school.

THE END